Lang Hyland was undeniably attractive;
he was also, equally undeniably, a womaniser—three months was the average life
of one of his ladies. Nicola was his secretary and that was all she intended to be;
she had no intention of being just another
scalp on Lang's belt. But would she have
the strength of mind to stick to her guns?

*Books you will enjoy*
*by CHARLOTTE LAMB*

## SAVAGE SURRENDER

Alex Lefkas was very handsome, charming, immensely rich—and accustomed to getting every woman he wanted. And he wanted Sophie. But Sophie wasn't like all those other women; she had no interest in Alex whatsoever—for she was protected from him by her undying love for another man. Or—was she?

## A FROZEN FIRE

For years Helen and Paul Eastwood's marriage had been a disastrous mockery. Paul was weak, vicious, blatantly unfaithful to her. But she was still his wife and some sense of duty still made her stay with him. But now Mark Eliot had come into her life. What would happen to her sense of duty now?

## CRESCENDO

'If you let them, women will take you over completely,' was Gideon Firth's philosophy—a philosophy that had as a result ruined Marina's life. And yet she went on loving him. Could she hope that Gideon's heartless attitude would change— or would she, eventually, come to her senses?

## STORM CENTRE

In bitter circumstances, five years ago Lauren had divorced her husband Andreas—and that was the end of that. But now, after an accident, Andreas had lost his memory and was asking for her, under the impression that she was still his wife. For his mother's sake, Lauren was forced to go through with the deception and go back to him—but how long could she stand the situation?

# OBSESSION

BY

## CHARLOTTE LAMB

**MILLS & BOON LIMITED**
15—16 BROOK'S MEWS
LONDON W1Y 1LF

*First published 1980*
*Australian copyright 1980*
*Philippine copyright 1980*
*This edition 1980*

© Charlotte Lamb 1980

ISBN 0 263 73330 0

*Set in Linotype Plantin 11 on 13 pt.*

*Made and printed in Great Britain by*
*Richard Clay (The Chaucer Press), Ltd., Bungay, Suffolk*

# CHAPTER ONE

NICOLA always walked to work. Her flat was in a side street in Chelsea, close to the river, and she liked to watch the Thames in all its changing moods as she walked. This morning, spring had whipped the water into a rolling torrent. Across the dark surface slid a wary sunshine, not sure whether it felt like shining or not. Nicola knew how it felt. She wasn't exactly dying to get to work this morning, either.

She had a cold. It had started this weekend and was now in full flood. She had made up very carefully this morning, but her face was pale and her nose showed a distinct tendency to be pink.

She walked quickly, pulling her fur collar close around her neck, but the wind managed to knife her through her warm winter coat. It was not going to be a good day. Apart from her cold, she had had a letter from her sister that morning. Caroline wanted to come to stay for a week, and the idea didn't give Nicola a thrill. Much as she loved her sister, she always felt easier when Caroline wasn't around. Caroline was unpredictable and Nicola did not feel strong enough today to face the prospect of trouble.

Their father had died when Caroline was six. It had left their mother alone to struggle, single-handed, with two girls and a small income. She had had to work, of course, and at times life had been difficult. 'While I'm not here, look after Caroline,' her mother had told Nicola. As the girls grew up, the theme song continued: 'Look after Caroline, Nicky. Don't forget, she's your little sister.'

How could Nicola forget? Caroline was always in trouble and Nicola was always having to get her out of it. Volatile, reckless, lighthearted, Caroline took risks which made Nicola wince. When their mother died, soon after Caroline's sixteenth birthday, Nicola faced the fact that her own adolescence was over. She was left alone to worry over Caroline.

Those teenage years had been a nightmare. Caroline had broken out of her schoolgirl chrysalis to become a ravishing, curvy blonde with eyes of a blue so dark that it seemed violet and no common sense at all. She took risks, as she always had, and now the risks gave Nicola a permanent haunted worry. The word no did not seem to be in Caroline's vocabulary. She dated the most unsuitable men and merely giggled when Nicola remonstrated with her about going to their flats or staying out at all-night parties. The two years between them seemed to stretch like elastic. Nicola felt very old by the time Caroline met David.

David was not merely a pleasant young man, he had his head screwed on soundly; he married Nicola's prize headache and took it away with him up north, liberating Nicola from four years of nervous tension.

But now Caroline, after a short two years of apparent bliss, had announced that she was coming to London. 'I'm bored stiff,' she had written, and Nicola had read the words with a sinking heart. Please, please, don't let her be bored with David, she had thought.

Turning into her office block, Nicola pushed the problem of her sister aside for later consideration. When she opened the door of her office she heard the quick, deep tones of her boss's voice followed by the slam with which he flung down the phone. Oh, dear, she thought. It's going to be one of those days, is it? Just what I needed. What else can go wrong?

She took off her coat and hung it in its usual place. As she was taking the cover off her typewriter the door was flung open. Reluctantly she looked round.

Lang Hyland confronted her across the office, black brows drawn together above his arrogant nose. Every time she saw him she was taken aback. He always seemed taller, leaner than she remembered: his black hair thicker, more vital, his features harder. Even after two years working for him, Nicola felt herself instinctively recoil from his forceful personality as from a blow.

'You're late. Where the hell have you been?'

She had learnt to count to ten before she answered him when he was in one of those moods. Her faint pauses sometimes gave her the presence of mind to smooth him down. One day, she was afraid, she would flare back at him.

'I'm sorry,' she answered now, quietly. 'I've got a cold and I overslept.'

'I've got a headache, but I still got here on time,' he retorted.

Nicola didn't answer that. Her blue eyes lowered to hide the look in them. If Lang Hyland had a headache he probably richly deserved one. He believed in burning the candle at both ends. He could hardly complain about the consequences.

He moved across the office at his usual rapid stride and leaned against the wall, looking out at the sky. The row of plants which Nicola cherished climbed towards the cold glass of the window as though searching for the invisible sun. Lang fingered a leaf absently. 'Got your pad?'

Nicola got it and sat down, waiting.

'Send a dozen red roses to Miss South,' he said.

'Red?' Nicola queried.

'Something wrong with your ears this morning?' he snapped. 'Dark red. You know the sort I mean.'

'Yes,' said Nicola, because she did, and she knew what it meant, too. Lois South was out. Her eyes flicked to the calendar. How long had she lasted? Christmas, she thought. It was Christmas when he picked her up. Nicola remembered because as soon as Lois South appeared she had been ordered to send dark red roses to his previous girl-friend. Nicola creased her brow. What had her name been? She couldn't remember, but the girl had been a blonde—a model, with a ravishing figure, and a vocabulary, as Nicola recalled it, of around six words, all of them apparently indicating yes.

Lois was a blonde, too. Nicola quite liked her, actually. Lois had rather more than six words but all the same her vocabulary also added up to yes.

He was a creature of habit. Men often were. He made lavish extravagant gestures at the beginning and end of his relationships; he sent the same flowers for the same reasons and he picked girls who had Identikit faces and bodies.

'Have you gone to sleep?' he demanded suddenly almost in her ear. 'Or are you hibernating?'

She looked round, startled, to find him right beside her. 'Sorry, Mr Hyland. Red roses for Miss South— I've got that.'

'If you're going to be useless you might as well have stayed at home,' he informed her. 'Get me my brother on the phone.'

He crossed the room like greased lightning, slamming the door. The glass in the panes rattled. Nicola winced, putting a hand to her head. She felt like putting out her tongue, but she was too old for that. You charming and delightful man, she thought. I just love working for you. I'd like to push you down the lift shaft

For a moment she dwelt on a fantasy of watching him vanishing with a wail, chuckling to herself, then she dialled Andrew Hyland's internal number and put him through.

Andrew, of course, was ultra-polite. 'How are you, Nicola? A cold morning. But I think the sun is trying to shine.'

'I've got a cold,' Nicola told him, and Andrew sounded sympathetic.

'Have you taken some aspirin?'

'I took one of those time capsule things.'

'I hope it works,' said Andrew. 'You shouldn't have come in today.'

Nicola said: 'But then Tricia would have had to work for Mr Lang.'

Andrew laughed and she put him through. Lang barked into the phone as usual as she put it down, and she grimaced at the receiver.

She rang the florist and the girl who took the call said knowledgeably: 'Oh, on her way out, is she?' She had worked there for several years and Lang Hyland was one of her best customers. She knew the signs too. 'Shall I put in the usual card?'

'Yes,' Nicola agreed. 'Just: Yours, Lang.'

'That's a laugh,' the girl said.

'Hilarious,' Nicola agreed as she put the phone down.

How did he do it? He hardly exuded charm, at least not in the office. Looks. Oh, yes, she thought, glancing at the closed door. He had those. And apparently wasn't ungenerous. Lois had got a diamond pendant; Nicola had chosen it herself. She wouldn't have been seen dead wearing it, but Lois had lit up like an electric light when Lang gave it to her. She had shown it to Nicola, unaware that Nicola had seen it before. 'Isn't it super?'

'Super,' Nicola had agreed, her face dead straight. In fact, she thought it rather vulgar, the design over-opulent, but she had chosen it with Lois's taste in mind, not her own, and apparently she had hit the nail right on the head. Lois had been glowing with delight.

Lang had stood listening, his face expressionless. Briefly, Nicola had met his eyes and seen dry irony in them. She had not shared the joke with him, looking away without registering the fact that she had seen and understood his amusement.

Afterwards, when Lois had gone, he had come back and looked oddly at Nicola. 'Would you have liked it?' he had asked.

'I don't care much for diamonds,' Nicola had told him.

'Have you ever been offered any?' he had asked, and he had been making fun of her, his face mocking.

'Not that I can remember,' Nicola had admitted calmly.

'And how would an offer be received?' he had asked, as though he knew the answer.

'With a kick in the teeth,' Nicola had said, meeting his eye.

He hadn't commented, merely walking away. She knew she was in no danger of getting an offer from him. Lang Hyland only went for blondes of a particular sort—long-legged, big-eyed, slightly empty-headed ones. He was rich enough to buy himself the toys he wanted and it was his life. Nicola had no views on the subject. The girls certainly did well out of it, as she was very well aware. Lang took them to the best clubs and restaurants. He gave them expensive presents. He sometimes took them abroad with him on business trips. He might be tough, terse and bloody-minded in the office, but maybe he wasn't like that in the bedroom. It always surprised Nicola the way they cried when he dropped them. They might have come out of it with some handsome diamonds, but they were by no means eager to let him go, and it wasn't just his money that attracted them.

No accounting for tastes, she thought, hearing his voice curtly giving his brother his orders for the day. If I were Andrew Hyland I'd be tempted to black his eye for him!'

When she first got the job she had been surprised to be told how many secretaries had come and gone in the previous year. She had only been there one day before she was thinking of handing in her notice herself.

Lang Hyland not only drove himself hard; he drove his colleagues into the ground trying to keep up with him. He had a source of personal energy which did not take into account any weakness in those who worked for him. He expected everyone to work as hard as he did. His hard, biting tongue was not spared if anyone fell short of his standards. His impatient temper pushed aside problems and cut through to the heart of the matter, seeing quickly and clearly where other people had puzzled for hours.

He was the core, the hub of the firm. The Hyland Property Company was based in London, but it had tentacles stretching out all over the country and across the continent. Property was a high risk area. It needed flair and intuition as well as a sound knowledge of the market's fluctuations.

Nicola had not expected to stay long during her first week. The curt commands, the impatient demand for speed, had been hellish. Lang had alarmed her so much she had been nervous all day. Gradually, though, she had learnt how to cope with him. Quiet, cool, capable, she had begun to run the office without losing her temper or becoming distraught, no matter how badly she was provoked. She might occasionally feel like picking up the wastepaper basket and emptying it over his head, but for all her reserved manner, Nicola had a sense of humour. She was able to laugh at Lang Hyland, even when his teeth snapped together and he snarled. It had saved her sanity and made it possible for her to do her job. He paid her so well that she was reluctant to find another job and, as the months went by, he had put her salary up several times, so that she thought twice before feeling like giving in her notice.

'Has the Grettan report shown any sign of turning up?' The question made her jump and Lang eyed her startled face with lifted brows. 'Were you daydreaming?'

'No, the report isn't in yet,' Nicola said, dragging her thoughts together.

'What the hell are they up to?' He came over to her desk and she involuntarily shifted away from the looming threat of his long body. Her thigh came in violent contact with her open desk drawer and she gave a yelp of agony.

'What have you done?'

'Nothing,' she muttered, surreptitiously massaging her leg.

Lang took hold of the back of her chair and swivelled her to face him. Before she could stop him he had gone down on one knee. As he brushed back her skirt, Nicola tried to pull it down again and Lang slapped her hand. He looked at the reddened mark on her thigh, touching it experimentally with one finger. 'Hurts?'

'Get your hand off me!' Nicola bit out.

'Don't be stupid, Nicky,' he said drily, looking up at her. He rarely used her first name and she didn't like it when he did. It made things far too personal. 'You'll have a terrific bruise there. Your skin shows every scratch, doesn't it? When you banged your arm on the door the bruise was there for weeks.'

She did not reply because she was too intent on trying not to blush. Lang's hand was moving soothingly over her thigh. He might not be aware of what he was doing, but Nicola was; very aware.

'That will teach you not to jump like a cat on hot bricks every time I come within an inch of you,' Lang murmured with amused satisfaction. He carefully drew her skirt down to her knee and rose, towering over her again. 'Where's the mail?'

She handed him the letters, her lips tight. Before he looked at them his glance shot to her face and he laughed outright. 'What an expression! There's no need to look as though I've outraged your virtue.'

'You wouldn't get the chance,' she muttered, head bent.

'What did you say?' He had tilted his black head and was trying to catch her mumbled words.

'Nothing,' she said, looking up, and then wishing she hadn't because there was a distinct gleam in his eye and she had a horrible suspicion he had heard precisely what she said.

He smiled at her, obviously amused, then began to skim through the letters in his hand. She watched him, following the strong line of his face from his deep forehead down the tough bones of his cheeks to that assertive, aggressive jaw. She was never sure where that impression of good looks came from—taken singly each of his features were more a revelation of power than of beauty. Yet the impression was left on one. His masculinity was overpowering, but the black lashes drooping against his cheek, the warm curve of his mouth, the clear hardness of his profile, gave pleasure to the eye.

Lang glanced up and Nicola hurriedly looked away.

'Lucci is giving a party this Saturday. You'd better come. Stick to me, and don't drink.'

'I'm sorry,' she said with an assumed calmness, 'it's impossible.'

'Impossible?' he repeated in a tone she knew only too well. It was the voice he used before he blew up.

'I'm really sorry, Mr Hyland,' she said quickly. 'I'll find someone else to go with you. Tricia, perhaps.' She hated sacrificing Tricia, who was petrified of him, but she had no option in this case. She couldn't spend the Saturday evening with him if Caroline was coming on the Saturday morning.

'If I wanted Tricia, I'd ask her,' he said unanswerably. 'Tricia never remembers a word. She has the most scrambled mind of any woman I've ever met.'

Only when Lang Hyland was within shouting reach, Nicola thought. Tricia's mind was perfectly adequate for anybody else.

'What are you doing at the weekend?' he demanded, staring at her.

Nicola hesitated, a faint obstinacy tightening her features. She was a slender, fine-boned girl with straight black hair which she wore in a simple style with a fringe across her forehead and the hair falling in a smooth frame around her face. Her usual expression was tranquil and thoughtful. Now she was frowning.

'I shall be busy,' she compromised. He had no right to know and she had no wish to tell him.

'A man?' he asked, still staring, and she caught the upward flick of his brows as though the idea amused him.

Nicola didn't answer, her pink mouth level.

'Is there a man in your life? I had the idea you were fancy free.' He watched her, leaning against her desk. 'Is it serious? You're not planning to get married, I hope? I know what happens when girls marry—they lose all interest in their job.'

Nicola ignored the questions. 'Can't Andrew go with you?'

'He can go,' Lang agreed with a slight dryness in his voice. 'But even if he stays as sober as a judge he'll never remember as clearly as you do.'

That could have been flattering if she hadn't already known it was the case. Lang wanted her there to monitor everything he said and did in case he forgot. He would be drinking. He wouldn't be able to avoid it. Although Lang didn't drink much normally he would be pressed to drink by Mr Lucci and to preserve the pretence of cheerful friendship he would have to accept.

'Bring your man along,' Lang suggested. 'I'd be interested to meet him. I didn't know he existed.'

Having solved that to his own satisfaction he returned to his own office and Nicola glared at his closed door. The telephone rang. She picked it up and Lois South's voice asked huskily, 'Is he in?'

Nicola heard the threat of tears in the other girl's voice. She knew perfectly well it was her cue to say he was out. Instead she murmured, 'Of course, Miss South,' and put the call through. She heard Lang say absently, 'Yes?'

'Oh, Lang!' Lois broke out, sobbing.

Nicola softly put down the receiver.

It didn't take him long. She had anticipated more of a breathing space. She heard the savage slam of the phone and then her door was pulled open.

She looked up with wide, innocent eyes.

Lang stared at her, his face alive with rage. 'Why did you put that call through?'

'You told me Miss South was always to be put through,' she answered softly, giving him a sweet smile.

He trod towards her desk with a tense prowling lope, like an animal, his eyes boring into her. 'All right,' he said. 'Is this some sort of campaign? What the hell's got into you this morning? You knew I wouldn't want to talk to her. I can't stand having women crying down phones at me.'

Nicola lowered her lashes. He can't stand it, she thought. Isn't that sad? He's so soft-hearted. He

doesn't mind breaking their hearts, but he can't bear
to hear them cry.

'You did it deliberately,' Lang accused.

'Why would I do that?' Nicola tried to stop herself
smiling, but the sound of her smile was in her voice.

His hands were planted on her desk. She looked up
in alarmed surprise. He was bending towards her, his
black head very close to her own, his face inches away.
It confused her to have him so near. She drew a shaky
breath and looked down again. Through almost closed
lips Lang asked softly: 'What's this all about?'

Nicola did what she always did when he was in a
menacing mood: she looked at him with a saccharine
smile. 'I'm sorry, Mr Hyland. I don't know what you're
talking about.' She used her softest voice, but his
face stayed hard.

'I always know when you're in a temper,' he said,
'because you start smiling like a crocodile and using
a voice like melted honey. At first I thought you were
just a simple-minded little bitch. Then I realised you
did it deliberately. And very effective it is, too. It's
hard to go on shouting at someone who smiles back
with sunny good temper and agrees with everything
you say.'

'I've never noticed it having any effect,' Nicola retorted before she had had time to think.

'Oh, yes, you have,' contradicted Lang. 'That's why
you do it. You know it takes the wind out of my
sails.' He paused. 'Why did you put Lois through
when you realised I'd ended it?'

'I must have forgotten,' Nicola murmured, her eyes shifting.

'Like hell! Try again, and this time try the truth. Was it a tit for tat because of your weekend plans? I told you, bring him along. He'll probably have the time of his life. Lucci always does these things well. There'll be champagne flowing like water and plenty of food.'

Giving up, Nicola said: 'It isn't a man. It's my sister.'

He raised one brow. 'Sister? I had the idea you were alone in the world.'

'Apart from Caroline, I am.'

'Caroline,' he said. 'Nice name. How old is she?'

'She's married,' Nicola said with a sudden sharpness.

Lang Hyland observed her, his hard eyes shrewd. 'I don't bite,' he said, and she knew he had picked up the intonation of her voice. She didn't want Caroline meeting him. Caroline was only too easily led astray, in Nicola's experience. And Caroline was also the sort of blue-eyed blonde Lang Hyland fancied.

'Bring her along,' he said.

Over my dead body, Nicola thought.

She was looking down, but she felt him watching her and wondered if he could read her expression. The idea of Caroline meeting up with Lang Hyland bred nightmares. Nicola valued her peace of mind too much. She didn't want her sister's marriage breaking up, nor did she want to have to sit and listen while Caroline wept brokenheartedly over her. In the past two years she had been forced to be a wailing wall for several of his discarded women. She didn't enjoy it, but she never had the heart to shut them up. His affairs never lasted and it was always Lang who ended them. Nicola couldn't remember an affair ending any other way. Three months, she thought; that was about average. In three months he could blast Caroline's life, and Nicola wasn't letting him do it.

'Does she look like you?' he asked. 'Is she older?'

To her relief the telephone rang. It was Lois again. With Lang watching her, Nicola lied smoothly and then had to listen as Lois asked her: 'Is there someone else? I didn't *do* anything. Oh, I'm so miserable! I love him.'

Nicola wished she hadn't become slightly friendly with her in the past; she wouldn't now have to listen to this. 'I'll tell him as soon as he comes back,' she promised. 'Yes, I know. Yes, I won't forget.'

When she had put the phone down, Lang straightened and gave her a nod of approval. 'That's better. I'm not in if she ever rings again. And don't pretend to forget again.' He moved away, whistling under his breath, and she looked at the back of his black head and wondered how it would feel to heave half a brick at it. She was just in the mood to do it this morning.

He shed his women like a dog shedding raindrops. It was none of her business, but it annoyed her. It might be the spring, or her cold, or Caroline's imminent reappearance in her peaceful life, but today she felt anarchic tendencies, a restless sensation of rebellion against fate.

Over the two years she had worked with him, she

and Lang had evolved a style of verbal shorthand which they used, a brief flash of comment between them which saved time. 'File,' he said. 'You answer that. I'll deal with this one.' They flicked through the pile of paperwork at a rapid speed. As he came to trust her, he had shifted a large part of the more routine of his work to her. The girls before her had never had access to the more private material, the confidential documents which rivals like the Lucci firm would give their eye teeth to know about. Nicola not only saw those reports. She often dealt with them in Lang's absence. She had the key to his secret files. Even his brother had never been allowed access to them.

Andrew popped his head round her door at one o'clock. 'Coming to lunch?'

She smiled at him and locked away the papers she had been working on before she joined him. They walked across the busy road, dodging between cars, and went into the restaurant they normally used.

Andrew wasn't quite as tall as his brother, but he was broader, his wide shoulders tapering to a slim waist. His hair was a dark brown, his eyes a pale blue. He was five years younger than Lang. A good, solid executive, Andrew could be trusted with anything, but he lacked Lang's flair and he certainly did not have his brother's tough fierceness of character.

Tricia, his secretary, said he was a lamb. 'Nothing like Lang.' Tricia had breathed it with relief. She hated coming into the office if Lang was around.

'How's Lang this morning?' Andrew asked.

'Wear your knuckledusters,' Nicola told him, and

they exchanged smiles of conspiratorial amusement. Although Nicola worked for his brother, not him, she saw a good deal of Andrew and they liked each other. They had discovered a mutual passion for sailing early on and this had bonded them, giving them an easy subject which could engross them for ages.

'Going to this Lucci affair?' Andrew asked.

'He wants me there.' She didn't actually say she was going because she was still debating it. She wasn't sure how Lang would react if she refused pointblank. He might be infuriating, but her salary was better than she could probably get elsewhere. She suspected Lang of having carefully edged her salary up as he realised they worked well together. She had become accustomed to that comfortable featherbedding. She didn't fancy taking a cut in salary if she moved on.

'I'm going,' said Andrew, smiling at her. 'It should be fun. Lucci always do their parties very well.'

'So Lang said,' Nicola murmured.

Despite their Italian-sounding name, Lucci were in fact an American-based firm who had sprung up in California. They were both rivals and allies of the Hyland firm, having worked closely with Lang sometimes in the past. Joe Lucci, the head of the firm, was a smiling monster with silvery hair and a very soft voice. Nicola did not like him. His son, Cary, was probably cut on the same pattern as his papa, but he was young enough to cloak it. He had almost effeminate good looks, loved clothes and women and was a frequent visitor to Lang's parties. Nicola met his smooth flatteries blankly; it was the easiest way of dealing with him. He had made a few passes at her when she first arrived but he had given up after a number of refusals. Like Lang, he preferred blondes, and he didn't waste his time if he thought he wasn't getting anywhere.

'Are you going for fun or as Lang's memory bank?' Andrew asked.

'His memory bank,' Nicola said flatly. Whenever Lang thought he might do business while he was drinking he took her with him to keep a careful track of what he said and promised.

'What would we do without you?' Andrew smiled. He had a strong face, his cheekbones broad, his eyes kind.

'Find somebody else,' Nicola told him, shrugging. 'Nobody is indispensible.'

'Lang would drive anybody else insane,' Andrew said drily.

'They would leave first,' she assented.

'You're the first who has lasted beyond three months,' said Andrew. 'They can't take it. You don't look tough, but you must be to last this long with him.'

Nicola had been very careful with what she said to Andrew at first, but she knew now that he never repeated her words to Lang. She trusted him.

'You need a sense of humour and good self-control,' she told him. 'I've promised myself that the day I leave the firm for good I'll tell your brother what I think of him.'

'And what's that?' asked a voice they both recognised.

Nicola stiffened. Andrew looked up in alarm.

'Oh, Lang,' he said, giving a quick placating smile. 'Having lunch? The steak is good, but don't have the mushrooms—I think they're off. We're just going. I must get the bill.'

Lang ignored him. He was standing behind Nicola. Although she didn't look round she could feel him there, vibrating like an engine at full throttle.

'You haven't answered me, Miss Adney,' he said close to her ear, bending down to speak very softly.

'We must go,' said Andrew, hovering. The waitress came past and he hailed her and began to pay the bill.

Nicola couldn't stand up without bumping into Lang, and he wasn't budging.

'Well?' he demanded.

Nicola drew a deep breath. She slid out of her chair sideways to avoid him and turned. 'I'll tell you the day I leave,' she said without meeting his eyes.

Andrew slid an arm round her waist almost protectively and they walked out while Lang stared after them.

# CHAPTER TWO

ON the Wednesday morning, she arrived for once to find Lang had not yet got to work. It was unusual for him. Although he apparently spent most of his leisure time in chasing blondes he still worked long, hard hours, frequently staying long after she had gone home and arriving before her in the morning. He ran on electricity, Nicola had decided long ago, plugging himself in overnight and waking up recharged and pulsating with power.

At ten o'clock Lois South arrived in a tidal wave of perfume and tears. She wept all over Nicola for a quarter of an hour. Since Lang hadn't arrived Nicola let her look in at his office, to prove she wasn't lying. The sight of his desk made Lois sob before she tottered away on her stilt-like heels. 'I never thought he would do this to me!'

Famous last words, Nicola thought as she closed the door on her. Poor Lois! She was a nice enough girl and basically very down-to-earth. She cooked like a dream, but Lang didn't like eating at home. He liked going out. He didn't want Lois getting that slippers-and-home-cooking feeling, Andrew said. It gave women ideas; ideas Lang Hyland didn't want entering their fluffy little heads.

Lang had the instincts of a jungle animal: keep free

of cages and keep your claws sharp. He prowled around the firm like a sleek tiger, seeing and hearing everything, constantly alert.

Andrew arrived at half past ten and looked incredulous when Nicola told him Lang hadn't yet arrived. Andrew based himself on a pattern of Lang but didn't have the teeth and claws for it. Instead he was a good right-hand man—clean-shaven, smooth-suited, every inch the eager young executive. At thirty, Andrew was somehow not quite mature. His manners were perfect, his intentions always good, but there was something hollow about him. He reminded Nicola of a chocolate Father Christmas she had once been given—it had looked solid and impressive, but when you picked it up, it was as light as air and empty inside.

'Hasn't he rung up?' he asked in disbelief.

'Not yet. Maybe his blonde is keeping him busy,' Nicola suggested drily.

'Is there one?' Andrew smiled.

'If he stays true to precedent,' Nicola shrugged. 'He usually drops one because he's found something more interesting.' Lang tired of his toys. They lost their novelty and he moved on.

The phone rang and Nicola answered it. 'You've given me your cold,' croaked a thick voice. 'I've got a sore throat and a splitting headache.'

She bit her lip, tempted to laugh. 'Oh, dear, I'm sorry.' She put her hand over the receiver and mouthed Lang at Andrew, who looked at her enquiringly.

'You'd better tell Andy to take over,' said Lang in a morose voice.

'He's here,' she said. 'I'll put him on.'

'He spends a lot of time in your office,' Lang accused. 'When I'm not there does any work get done?'

Without replying she handed the phone to Andrew and listened as he exclaimed sympathetically and asked if there was anything he could do, then listened and nodded as Lang *told* him what he could do.

After a few minutes he handed her the phone again. 'Get round here,' Lang muttered. 'And bring the mail.' He dropped the phone and she winced. So that was what it felt like to have that man slam phones down on you. Not a pretty sensation.

'What a cheerful mood he's in,' she commented to Andrew.

'Colds do make one feel glum,' Andrew said at once.

'So they do,' Nicola agreed, smiling.

She took a taxi to Lang's flat. When he said now he meant half an hour ago and soon meant faster than the speed of light. He was paying for the taxi, anyway.

When he opened the door his hair was dishevelled, his jaw unshaven and blurred with shadow, his skin pale. To her embarrassment he was wearing a short, dark blue towelling robe and only too obviously nothing else. His long legs were bare, the dark hairs rough on their skin, and Nicola felt a strange alarmed quiver of realisation as she glanced at them. Had he been about to shower? Or didn't he wear anything in bed?

She looked up and Lang eyed her narrowly. 'Well? Are you going to stand there all day?'

She walked past him, saying hurriedly: 'Andrew sends his sympathies.'

'Does he?' There was a terse flatness about that. He closed the door and followed her down the hall. A room on the left showed her his tumbled bed. Nicola walked past the open door towards the lounge.

'I'm going back to bed,' Lang informed her back.

She halted and looked round, but he had vanished. Slowly and with great reluctance she went back to the door of his bedroom. He was now in the bed and to her relief he was still huddled in the blue robe.

'God, I feel awful,' he groaned as she stood there looking warily at him. 'Oh, come in, I shan't bite. I haven't had a cold for years.'

Nicola advanced and hovered, wondering whether to sit down or not. Lang leant over and grabbed a paper tissue from a box on his bedside table. His bed, she noticed, was king-size and draped with a silk quilt cover the colour of sand. The bed linen was a chocolate brown and matched the curtains. They were drawn back. Daylight streamed into the room, showing her Lang's pallor and gloomy expression.

He was sneezing and swearing at the same time. As he grabbed another tissue Nicola saw his blue robe part, the movement revealing the smooth brown skin of his collarbone, the short dark hair roughening his chest. She looked away.

'You gave me this,' he accused.

'I'm sorry, it wasn't deliberate,' she said, and got the full force of one of his glares.

'I wouldn't put it past you.'

Her eyes opened wide in surprise. Was he serious?

He was looking at her with brooding irritation, his brows knitted in a scowl.

'Where's the mail?' he demanded, and she handed it to him. She had already skimmed through it, removed all the stuff he wouldn't need to see and he only had to glance through the rest.

'Andrew and I can deal with it all.'

'Can you now?' His voice was dry, he threw her a look from under his dark lashes. 'You're too damned sure of yourself, Miss Adney.'

Nicola made no attempt to answer that. He sneezed again and gave up his attempt to read the letters, shoving them all back at her.

'All right, deal with it, then. Anything urgent? You'll have to cancel all my appointments.'

'I've already done so.'

'Don't exceed your brief, Miss Adney,' he rapped out. 'Wait until I give you your orders in future, will you?'

'Yes, sir.' She said it with a broad smile and he met her eyes with a distinct snap of his teeth.

'Stop smiling at me! You may think this funny, but I damned well don't. I can't stand being ill.'

'You're not ill, Mr Hyland. You've just got a cold.'

'I'll say whether or not I'm ill,' he said in that thickened voice. 'My throat's like a cheese grater and my head keeps exploding when I sneeze. I think I've got a temperature.'

'You look pale, if anything,' she told him.

He didn't like that. 'Feel my forehead,' he demanded.

Nicola just looked at him.

'Go on, feel it,' he insisted. 'I'm burning with fever.'

Gingerly, she laid her hand on his forehead. It felt perfectly normal to her. 'No, I'm sure you haven't got a temperature.'

'Damn you, I know I have!' he exploded. 'Get a thermometer.'

She had not believed he would become so childish in illness. She looked at him with sheer disbelief. 'Oh, well, if you want to have a temperature, have one.'

He regarded her as if he wanted to throttle her. 'I tell you, I'm ill. Why are you pretending there's nothing wrong with me?' He lay back against the great pile of untidy pillows, glowering. 'Why don't you do something? You haven't got a womanly bone in your body, have you? Lois would be making hot lemon and whisky by now or soothing my fevered brow, not looking at me as though I were a mental case.'

'Shall I ring her?' Nicola suggested.

'God, no,' he said, revolted by the idea. 'You think I want to give her a chance to get her foot over the threshold?'

'Where's Preston?' she asked, suddenly realising his manservant hadn't put in an appearance.

'Gone to Blackpool to visit that deaf sister of his— they sit and shriek at each other about old times until they can't stand the sight of each other and part for another year.' Lang sneezed again and Nicola detached a tissue from his box and handed it to him.

He took it, his grey eyes lifting to her face. 'I'm

all alone,' he said pathetically.

'Shall I ring your sister?' she asked, visited by a brilliant idea. His sister, Monica, was married to a Harley Street surgeon and lived in a large house in Buckinghamshire. She was a brisk, acquisitive lady with two sons, a daughter, two dogs and a canary, a large white horse and a sleek sports car. When she visited the London office Lang always did a disappearing act. Monica had shares in the firm and liked to keep a close eye on their movements. She regarded her brothers as personal property and kept a close eye on their movements, too. Nicola found her amusing in small doses. Monica's brain was as sharp as Lang's and her eyes as piercing.

'God forbid,' he said piously. 'I'm too ill to put up with Monica.' He lowered his lashes and watched her through them. 'Make me a hot drink.' He sounded like a little boy and she observed him with dry suspicion. Lang was up to something. Her eyes took in the pallor again, the roughness of his unshaven skin. Whatever he was up to, he wasn't well, although he was clearly exaggerating it.

His kitchen was a miracle of modern gadgets. Preston evidently expected the best. Nicola found some lemons and squeezed them, heated water and mixed the two, adding a generous finger of whisky, some sugar and, finally, the juice of an orange.

Lang was sitting up against his pillows, reading the pink pages of the *Financial Times*, but he accepted his whisky and lemon with alacrity.

'Is there anything else?' she asked.

'Stop trying to leave! My bed's uncomfortable. Could you remake it for me?'

He went off to the bathroom while she remade his bed. One of his pillows dropped to the floor. She bent to pick it up and jumped as the phone rang by his bed.

It was Lois, and she sounded shrill as she asked if Lang was there. 'He's ill, Miss South,' Nicola told her soothingly.

'Why are you there?' Lois had suspicion in her voice.

'I brought him the letters. I'll tell him you rang.'

As she put the phone down Lang padded barefoot into the room. Nicola averted her eyes while he climbed into bed again, sighing with pleasure at the neatness of it.

'That's better,' he approved. 'Who was that on the phone?'

'Lois.'

'God.' He caught her eye and grimaced. 'Why do women never know when something's over?'

'Why do they ever start it?' Nicola muttered as she turned away.

'What?' Lang demanded.

She didn't answer, walking towards the door.

'Where are you going? Come back here. I'm hungry. And I've probably got pneumonia.'

'You haven't got pneumonia. A slight cold, that's all that's wrong with you,' Nicola informed him impatiently.

'Is that all the sympathy I'm going to get?' He lay

back on his pillows, his black hair tousled, his face pale, and looked sulky.

The phone rang again. 'If that's Lois, I've lost my voice.'

It was Lois, and she didn't believe a syllable of Nicola's gentle explanation. Lang watched as Nicola lied and she caught his grin out of the side of her eye and felt like hitting him.

'You didn't tell me that before!' Lois screeched.

'It was coming on,' Nicola hedged. 'Now he's too hoarse to talk.'

'He can listen,' Lois said unanswerably. 'Put him on—I've got a few words to say to him.'

Nicola looked at Lang and he pulled the bedclothes over his head. 'He's gargling in the bathroom,' Nicola said, and Lois began to use language which made Nicola's hair curl. Lois had always seemed quite a pleasant girl, but her vocabulary was more extensive than Nicola had suspected. Nicola couldn't disagree with the description of Lang. He was a lying, lowdown bastard.

'You're welcome to him,' Lois informed her with loathing. 'Make sure you get something out of him now or you never will.' She hung up and Lang emerged to give Nicola a coaxing little smile to which she gave a frozen stare in return.

'Would you mind telling your ex-flame that I haven't supplanted her, please? I don't want rumours of that sort starting up.'

Lang looked surprised, then laughed. 'Oh, is that what she thinks?'

'Just tell her, would you?' Nicola eyed him and thought that she could give Lois a few tips on vivid descriptions of him, and she wouldn't have to resort to four-letter words.

'If I ever see her again, I'll tell her,' he agreed with the blatant proviso that he had no intention of seeing Lois again.

'I'm starving,' he pleaded. 'My throat's sore and I couldn't eat anything solid. When I was little, my mother used to give me bread and milk when I had a sore throat.'

'Bread and milk? I think I could manage that,' Nicola said at once.

He looked aghast. 'I think I'd prefer scrambled eggs,' he told her hurriedly. She had known he didn't want bread and milk—the reference to him being little was supposed to soften her, make her feel womanly and maternal towards him. Some hope, she thought, looking at him with scathing distaste. Bread and milk! He obviously hated the stuff. Hot lemon and whisky was more his mark.

He eyed her through his lashes, a faint impatience in the line of his mouth. 'I'm ill. I haven't had a thing to eat since last night and I feel faint with hunger.'

'You can't be very ill if you're hungry.'

The lashes flickered on his cheek. He really was pale, she thought, looking at the rough unshaven texture of his skin. He lifted his eyes and smiled coaxingly at her again.

'Some scrambled eggs and some coffee, please,' he asked.

He was turning on charm suddenly. It lay in the grey eyes, in the coaxing mouth, and Nicola looked away. She could look at him blankly when he roared and stamped around the office, but she found his deliberate, teasing charm disturbing. There was no way she was going to get out of here until she had cooked him a meal, so she shrugged, and walked off to the kitchen.

She made tiny snippets of thin toast with the scrambled egg and served it on a pretty plate, the toast surrounded the egg, the whole sprinkled with finely chopped chives. It had amused her to see the row of potted herbs along the windowsill. Preston was a man who took his work seriously, obviously. She identified rosemary, basil and thyme, sniffing them with appreciation.

Lang was buried in his paper again and surfaced to accept the tray, throwing a quick glance over the food. 'Very pretty,' he congratulated her. She slipped out while he ate and came back to find he hadn't left so much as a scrap of egg. He drank the creamy coffee she had made him and then snuggled back like a child under the bedclothes. If he expected her to tuck him in and fuss over him, he was going to be disappointed, Nicola thought, watching.

'You'd feel better if you wore pyjamas,' she pointed out.

'Top drawer,' he told her at once, pointing to the chest on the far side of the room.

She looked drily at him and went over to find them. The top pair was fine silk, a deep maroon shade. She flipped them over, but the others were equally impracticable. In the end she handed him a pair of the silk ones and he started undoing his robe. Nicola shot out of the room and heard him laughing, quite distinctly. He called her back a moment later. When she returned she told him she must go. Lang lay back and shrugged.

'Very well, go,' he said, as though accusing her of something.

'I've got such a lot of work to do.'

Why was she apologising, for heaven's sake? He paid her to run his office, not to hang around his flat nursing him over a slight cold.

'That's all right,' he said, still reproachful.

As she opened the door to leave he said: 'Call in on your way home and tell me if the Grettan Project report turns up.'

'Yes,' she said, nodding.

'And bring me a list of any telephone calls,' he added quickly as she turned to go. 'I might have some dictation for you to type out tomorrow.'

'I should forget about work for a few days,' she said.

'Do as you're told.'

He was sounding more himself and Nicola found that reassuring. She shrugged and went. Andrew was in Lang's chair at Lang's desk and looking very uneasy about it. They worked together for the rest of the day and she went back to Lang's flat with a list of messages that evening.

When he let her in, he was back in his robe again, but this time he had clearly just had a shower. He was carrying a towel with which he rubbed his head as he walked up the hall. There was an electric log fire burning in the lounge and some jazz playing on his stereo. He had been drinking whisky again, she noted, eyeing the empty glass. A copy of *The Economist* lay open on the carpet beside it.

She handed him the typed list of messages. He scanned it briefly, then handed it back. 'Grettan report in?'

She shook her head.

'You're obviously feeling better,' she suggested, and he gave her an ironic little smile.

'Oh, you approve of that, do you?'

She met his eyes with stone-walling blankness, not quite sure about this new mood of his, and he laughed shortly. 'How's Andrew coping?'

'Admirably.'

'Isn't that nice,' he said, his black head tilted to one side, his mouth crooked. His skin had been shaved recently and was still slightly damp from his shower. His colour was better, but his eyes were sharp. 'Going to cook me a meal?'

'Do I get overtime?' She wished she hadn't said it as soon as it flew out, but it was too late and Lang's eyes sparked angrily.

'Services above and beyond the call of duty? Of course. How much do you want?' His tone was barbed and Nicola sighed.

'It was a joke.'

'I'm hysterical.'

'Why don't you go back to bed?' she said wearily,

because she still had the lingering remnant of her own cold and she had had a difficult day. He was too much at six o'clock on a chilly spring day.

He turned and went and she cooked him some fish from the deep freeze compartment. After that she made his bed again while he watched her, and didn't quite like the way he did it, his narrowed grey eyes observing every movement, the stretch of her body across the bed, the black hair falling forward across her face as she bent down. He didn't say a word, but Nicola was tense. There was insolence in his eyes as she turned to face him.

'If you were taller, you'd have a perfectly proportioned body,' he commented, making her skin burn. 'You're just a shade on the thin side.'

'I do apologise,' Nicola snapped.

Her anger amused him further. He got into the bed and as she left called: 'Come at ten tomorrow.'

She didn't answer, very tempted to slam the front door as she walked out of his flat. She was well aware that she had just been stripped visually by an expert. She had felt his eyes on her every second of the time while she made that bed. It wasn't the first time he had deliberately annoyed her by inspecting her like that, but she had thought he had stopped doing it. At first, during her early months with him, it had been one of his regular ways of getting under her skin, but gradually as they began to work so well together, he had dropped it.

Probably he was in a mischievous mood because he wasn't too well and feeling awkward. All the same, she could have hit him. He used his sexual power as a weapon; Nicola knew that. She had seen him do it. Most women looked addled when Lang turned his grey eyes on them with the deliberate intention of making them aware of him sexually. Nicola merely felt a mixture of uneasiness with irritation.

In the office next day she mentioned to Andrew that Lang was in a difficult mood and he asked, staring at her: 'You don't like him much, do you?'

'I'm not one of his fans.'

'Funny, that. Most women fall like ninepins.'

'That's because they don't work for him. Ask Tricia if she thinks he's sexy and charming.'

Andrew's pale eyes lit with amusement. 'I know Tricia's terrified of him.'

'Whatever charm he has, he doesn't waste it on us,' Nicola shrugged. 'He's clever and I have to admit he works like a beaver, but he's not a comfortable man to have around.'

She went over to his flat at ten and found him blinking sleepily, having been woken by her arrival. He hadn't even combed his hair and it stood up in thick untidy peaks. He hadn't shaved and he was still wearing that robe and no pyjamas.

'Get me some breakfast, will you?' he commanded, disappearing into the hall.

Nicole followed to protest and he turned. 'I'm going to the bathroom. Where are you going?'

She stopped and he gave her a glinting look and vanished. Nicola said something under her breath. She didn't often swear, but she had promised Andrew she would get back to the office by eleven to sit in on a round table discussion with the men who had been doing the Grettan report.

She had just got him his breakfast when she heard him emerge from the bathroom. She made the mistake of going out of the kitchen. He was now wearing just a towel wrapped round his waist; the smooth skin of his shoulders gleamed wetly. Nicola caught his glance and hurriedly withdrew again.

He was using her as free domestic help and she resented it. When was Preston coming back? she wanted to know.

She gave Lang a few moments to get dressed and then went towards the bedroom. She tapped on the door, the tray in her hand, and he called: 'Come in,' but when she opened the door he was still wearing nothing but the towel, standing in front of his dressing-table, brushing his hair. In the mirror their eyes met. Nicola felt herself turning pink.

'Put it down on the bed,' Lang said. He was still husky, but his voice had improved a good deal over the last twenty-four hours. There was a freshly opened box of tissues beside the bed, so obviously he had been using them up at a tremendous rate.

'I took one of those capsules. It seems to have worked.' He turned and watched her as she put down the tray.

She turned and he had moved over towards her. Nicola had a peculiar sensation of confusion as their eyes met. He was so tall, his body so powerful, and she knew she was blushing violently.

'Where's your robe?' she asked in a hurried, husky voice.

'What's the matter?' Lang drawled, laughter in his voice. 'Haven't you ever seen a man without his clothes on before? What an interesting thought!'

She was furious with the taunt in his voice. Stung, she glared at him. 'Get something on!'

'My God,' Lang jeered, 'I do believe you're a virgin.'

Heat was burning in her face and her eyes were a violent, dark blue. She turned to shoot out of the room and Lang caught her arm and held her, struggling, not hurting her but imposing his strength to stop her escaping.

'Let go of me,' she muttered, tugging at her arm. Her eyes flicked to him and away as she took in the smooth, bare shoulders, the deep dark-haired chest. He had muscles she hadn't suspected. His arms were powerful, his naked thighs strongly moulded. He was staring at her with narrowed eyes which glimmered with amusement.

'Are you frightened of me?'

'No,' she lied shakily. 'I'm just annoyed. Let go!'

'What do you imagine I might do, I wonder?' Lang laughed under his breath as she tensed and renewed her efforts to get away. His other hand came up to cup her chin. She tried to wrest her head away but couldn't move it. Lang bent forward and brushed his mouth lightly, teasingly, over her lips. 'There,' he said with mockery. 'You can stop trembling. It's over.'

She was released. Lang turned to the bed and Nicola

fled from the room in total disarray. In the kitchen
she leant on the wall. Her face was so hot she had to
splash it with cold water before she could summon
the nerve to go back to him.

He had eaten his breakfast and was dressed in a
cream fisherman's sweater and pants. He gave her a
wicked grin as she walked into the room. 'Feel better
now?'

'I must go,' she said, ignoring that.

'You'll have to take Andrew to the Lucci party,'
Lang told her.

'You aren't going?'

He shook his head. 'I think I'll take the weekend
off.'

Nicola left for the office, still fuming. The little inci-
dent bothered her. It was the first time Lang had ever
behaved like that with her. He had been amusing himself with her. She wasn't his type and he knew she
didn't fancy him, either, but the devil finds work for
idle hands to do. Lang had been bored alone in his
flat all day. He was nowhere near as ill as he chose
to believe, and he had turned his potent sexual weapons
on her for amusement. She could kick herself for having let him get under her skin, even briefly.

'I'll pick you up at your flat to take you to the party,'
Andrew offered as she left that evening.

'Would you mind if my sister came?' Nicola asked.
'She's only in London for a week and I don't like to
walk out on her on her first evening here.'

'Delighted,' he said, smiling at her. 'Is she older
than you? She's married, didn't you say?'

'She's married, but she's two years younger.'

'Is she like you?'

Nicola laughed. 'Wait and see.' Andrew was in for a surprise when he saw Caroline. There wasn't any resemblance between her and Nicola at all. Their mother had been dark, but their father had been a fair-skinned blond and it was his looks that Caroline had inherited.

Caroline sauntered off the train next morning, a picture of elegance, wearing a very expensive suit and a black hat. Behind her staggered a bemused young man carrying her cases. Caroline greeted Nicola with a wave and dismissed her ardent admirer with a few sweet words.

'Caroline!' Nicola sighed as she kissed her. Anyone looking at them would imagine that it was Caroline who worked in London for a worldwide firm and Nicola who was a harassed wife.

'London,' Caroline smiled, looking around her with bright, eager blue eyes. 'London! I can hardly believe it.'

'You only live just over a hundred miles away,' Nicola pointed out. 'Hardly the back of beyond.'

'I haven't been to town or seen any real shops for years!'

'Where did you buy that? Woolworths?' Nicola eyed her from head to toe with admiring irony.

Caroline shrugged her slender shoulders with an economic and graceful gesture. 'You've no idea how bored I am.'

'How's David?'

Caroline ignored that. 'I'm going to enjoy myself while I'm here.'

Nicola's heart sank. 'Oh, are you?' she asked as she looked at her sister's exquisite profile under the black hat.

Caroline was delighted by the news about the Lucci party. She pumped Nicola for information about the people who would be there and was obviously very interested in both young Lucci and Andrew, until Andrew arrived and she cast a shrewd eye over him and recognised that he was not the sort of man to make passes at married women.

Andrew looked astounded as they shook hands. He looked over Caroline's sleek figure as he spoke to her in his careful, polite way. She was wearing a backless satin dress in a muted shade of coffee. It left little of her curves to the imagination. Nicola wondered how David managed to afford such clothes for her and grimly hoped Caroline wasn't in as reckless a mood as she suspected. Caroline had altered in the past two years. She looked sophisticated, very daring in her skimpy dress, and she looked very expensive to keep.

Nicola was making no effort to compete. She was wearing her black dress, the one she usually wore to these occasions. It made her both presentable and almost invisible. Sleeveless, the bodice had a tight, shirred fall to her small waist and the skirt clung smoothly, emphasising her slender hips. Nobody was going to be noticing her.

Andrew had got them both flowers, to her surprise. He gave Caroline a creamy carnation with a glittering gold ribbon bow from which trailed a short cluster of gold ribbons, but to Nicola he smilingly handed a white one with silver ribbons. 'I must have known,' he said as he watched her pin it at the side of her hair.

Caroline got him to pin hers to her bodice, and Andrew's ears went red as he fumbled with her dress and he was obviously glad to complete the task.

Caroline gave him an acid little look, dismissing him from her list of possible conquests.

She had a distinct glint in her eye as they arrived at the party. The Lucci family had taken a large saloon in a famous London hotel. Soft-voiced Papa Lucci came to greet them. He smiled caressingly at Caroline, but it was to Nicola he turned his real attention. Nicola was always at Lang Hyland's elbow; Papa Lucci didn't waste his flatteries on someone without influence.

Cary was less single-minded. When Nicola detached herself from his father's purring attempts to coax information out of her, she saw Caroline and Cary drinking together, tête-à-tête in a corner.

She moved to break that up and Andrew unluckily joined her. He wanted to tell her she looked charming. Nicola could have hit him. She had wanted to whisk Caroline away, but Andrew and Cary launched into a conversation and Caroline stuck to them like glue.

Cary was glancing at her all the time, his white teeth gleaming. He didn't have to say that Caroline was enchanting; his bright eyes said it all the time.

It didn't do him any good in the long run, though, because to Nicola's horror Lang Hyland suddenly arrived. Nicola hadn't seen him walk in and when she heard his voice behind her, her heart took a nose dive. Oh, no, she thought, not him! She looked at Caroline with anxious concern, but Caroline was already gazing at him and her blue eyes were avid.

'Aren't you going to introduce me to your sister, Nicola?' Lang enquired softly behind her.

Caroline's lashes flickered over her smooth cheeks. She wasn't actually smiling, but she looked like a cat that has swallowed the cream.

Nicola turned her head slowly, met Lang's eyes and saw cool amusement in them. He was here deliberately. He had lied to her when he said he was too ill to come to this party. He had wanted her to bring Caroline and had suspected she wouldn't if he was going to be there.

All these realisations flashed through her mind even as she was staring blankly at him.

All of it had been a well-thought-out plan. His cold had given him the perfect excuse. She had known he was exaggerating his symptoms, but it had never entered her head that he had been doing it with malice aforethought.

She introduced him to Caroline and Lang stepped forward to take Caroline's hand.

They looked at each other with frank assessment. Lang was in evening dress, and he looked superb. It infuriated Nicola to admit that. He looked taller than ever, the tough handsome face faintly mocking, his mouth curved in a sensual twist as he looked at Caroline.

Nicola had known it would happen if they met. She watched it with stoic irony.

Caroline fluttered her artificial black lashes at him and laughed. 'So you're Nicky's boss!'

'Does she give me a good report?' he asked, and his eyes flicked to Nicola because he knew she wouldn't have done and that amused him. He gave her a quick, wicked smile which she did not return.

He looked back at Caroline. All the boredom had gone from her exquisitely made up features. She was very much alive now and she was making no attempt to hide the fact that she fancied Lang Hyland very much indeed. Nor was he making any secret of the fact that it was mutual.

I've got to stop it, Nicola thought grimly. But how?

# CHAPTER THREE

THE thing that annoyed her most was that Lang Hyland was amused. Although he was flirting with Caroline on and off for the rest of the evening, he kept Nicola at his side and forced her to be an unwilling witness, his grey eyes gleaming with laughter whenever she met them. He knew exactly what was going on inside her head. Her impotent anger appeared to be giving him a lot of pleasure, judging from the way he grinned whenever she turned her glance in his direction.

It wasn't news to her, of course, that he had a sense of humour. He had revealed it on other occasions. But Nicola didn't like knowing that he was laughing at her.

It occurred to her that in a way she had brought this about herself. When he questioned her about Caroline she had been foolish enough to betray to him her desire that he shouldn't meet her sister, and, being Lang Hyland, he had not been slow to work out why. He had probably guessed that Caroline was attractive. Why else should Nicola have wanted to stop them meeting?

She had noticed before that he had a tendency to tease. He had often deliberately teased Lucci Senior by talking to her in front of the old man in veiled terms which left Lucci dying to know what Lang had been talking about.

'You didn't tell me your sister was a raving beauty,' he accused when they were alone for a moment.

'Caroline is married and not available,' Nicola countered with conscious optimism.

Lang's brows flew up. 'She looks pretty available to me.' The infuriating thing about that was that he was dead right—Caroline had been giving him a strong come-on ever since she met him. She couldn't have been more obvious if she had had it written in neon lights on her forehead.

'Caroline hasn't got any sense,' Nicola muttered.

'Or she wouldn't flirt with me?' Lang watched her, grey eyes gleaming with amusement. 'Have you ever given anyone the green light, Nicky? Or do they all get the no-sale sign you give me?'

'I wasn't aware I gave you any signs at all,' she retorted.

'Oh, yes, you were,' he drawled smoothly. 'You know precisely what you're doing.'

Cary Lucci drifted up to them, giving Lang a nod before turning his flattering dark eyes on Nicola. 'You haven't tried our caviar yet. Come and tell me what you think of it.'

Lang's hand snaked out and caught her waist, drawing her against his side. 'She isn't hungry,' she heard him tell Cary in a lazy, smiling voice which yet conveyed decision.

Cary's father was hovering nearby, waiting to get Lang alone. He had been trying all evening without success. Lang hadn't let Nicola leave him for a second.

Cary looked meltingly into Nicola's eyes and gave her his party special: the smile he knew from experience turned girl's heads.

'Just taste the caviar, Nicky,' he suggested, winding his fingers through hers and giving her a little tug.

He really was a charmer in a totally artificial way. He could be a delightful, amusing companion if you didn't take him seriously. Nicola gave him back the smile, her eyes laughing.

'Another time, Cary.'

'Please, Nicky,' said Cary, pulling at her.

Lang's hand tightened. She looked up and found him eyeing her ironically. She was tempted to go with Cary just to annoy him, and Lang caught the flicker of rebellion in her eyes and smiled again, his expression warning her not to give in to impulse.

Mr Lucci oiled in as reinforcements to his son. 'You're not dieting, are you, Nicola? You certainly don't need it.' His silvery hair shone under the lights as he blandly inspected her with flattering interest.

Completely unflattered, Nicola shook her head. 'Just not hungry,' she shrugged.

'A pity,' Cary mourned, still trying to woo her with his smile.

'Yes, isn't it? Never mind, the champagne is delicious,' Nicola smiled.

Cary withdrew, defeated. Mr Lucci stood talking to Lang and Nicola for ten minutes, getting nowhere, and then moved off in search of easier prey.

Lang glanced down at Nicola. His arm was still

round her waist and now that they were safely alone she wriggled free. He gave her a wry smile. 'Cary Lucci fancies you, doesn't he?'

'Cary Lucci fancies a lot of women.' Nicola knew Cary thought her attractive and her voice was cool. She had no intention of letting him sleep with her, and that was all Cary Lucci would have in mind if she encouraged him.

'But you don't fancy him?' Lang had lifted one dark brow and was smiling slightly, his eyes narrowed.

Nicola looked away, suddenly oddly hot. She hadn't drunk much and although the room was crowded it hadn't seemed so airless a moment ago. Deliberately, she shrugged her shoulders. 'He's very good-looking.'

There was a little silence. She looked up quickly and Lang was watching her with an expressionless face. 'How well do you know him?' he asked, and Nicola felt herself growing hotter.

Did Lang imagine that she was secretly dating Cary? He wouldn't like that, she realised. Lang had gradually, over the two years she had worked for him, come to trust her with some of his very private information and he would not be pleased if he suspected she was seeing Cary Lucci.

Before she had time to answer his question, he asked another, his tone hard. 'Why are you blushing?' His grey eyes pierced her face. 'Is he your lover?'

The terse question broke her alarmed suspension. 'No, he isn't,' she snapped back. 'And never likely to be. Cary Lucci is a womaniser and I don't happen to fancy being one of a procession.'

Lang's face relaxed and he gave her a sardonic grin. 'That was what I thought, but women are deceptive. You're more Andrew's type.'

'What type is that?'

'Sweet, virginal,' Lang mocked.

Her cheeks burnt. 'One day——' she started, and stopped hurriedly.

'One day what?' he enquired, his eyes lazy.

She didn't answer.

'Is this another message I'm going to get the day you leave?' Lang asked in pretended interest. 'I can't wait.'

Nicola lifted her glass and drank the rest of her champagne, while Lang watched, smiling.

'Just remember, young Lucci is only interested in you because you work for me. Keep him at a distance.'

'I'm not stupid!'

'Not stupid,' he agreed. 'But female. And they tend to lose their heads when a good-looking boy like that turns the heat on.'

'Not me,' Nicola said with certainty. 'He doesn't turn me on.'

'Does anyone?' The soft question threw her into disturbed confusion. She felt his eyes moving over her from her straight, sleek hair to her feet. 'You see a lot of Andrew, don't you? He's always in your room. You lunch with him, too. Does Andrew turn you on?'

She shrugged, not answering.

'But you haven't slept with him yet.' Lang made that a statement, his eyes intent, and Nicola flared angrily.

'That's all you think there is to it, isn't it?'

Lang shot her a strange, sharp look, his black lashes shifting against the hard angle of his cheekbone. 'Does it add up to more for you and Andrew?' His voice was curt and Nicola felt herself stiffen. He was wondering if she hoped to marry Andrew, she realised, and Lang clearly didn't like that idea. Her spine tingled with anger as she took in the implications of that. Lang was prepared to smile cynically on a temporary liaison, but he wasn't going to have his brother being lured into marriage. Nicola was not suitable as a wife for one of the Hyland family.

She forced herself to look calm, not betraying the rage she felt. 'Ask Andrew,' she said.

'Oh, I will,' Lang warned softly. He gave her another of those insolent, stripping glances and Nicola's hands curled at her side impotently. The grey eyes held a gleaming curiosity as they wandered from her bare pale shoulders down the whole length of her body in the clinging black dress. When they came back to her face Lang took in the chilly expression she wore and began to laugh. 'Andrew must have more to him than I'd imagined if he can get through your armour!'

Nicola gathered together her dissolving sense of humour. She would not let him taunt her into losing her temper. Sweetly, smiling, she retorted: 'Well, you can't be right all the time.'

'But I work at it,' Lang assured her, still amused. A waiter passed and he reached out a hand to take a glass from his tray. Nicola watched his white cuff shoot back, the sinewy wrist exposed, darkened by short rough hair. He turned back and their eyes met. Nicola hurriedly looked away.

Andrew had been hovering nearby, staying at a distance because whenever Lang caught sight of him he silently warned him to stay where he was while he was talking to Nicola. Andrew obediently waited. Lang threw him a sardonic look now. 'Shall I give him a whistle for you?'

Nicola could have hit him. He didn't need to underline Andrew's faithful obedience to him. Andrew was not merely fond of his brother; he admired him, even if he was aware of Lang's shortcomings. In Nicola's opinion, Lang underestimated Andrew. Because his brother did not have his own driving force, he shrugged him aside, and he was wrong. Andrew saw Lang far more clearly than Lang perhaps knew, and if Andrew recognised in Lang a ruthless disregard for ordinary scruples, he still admired him for his brains and ability.

'I can give my own whistles,' she told Lang, moving away from him. As soon as she left Lang, Andrew joined her, a smile on his face, and behind her she heard Lang laugh softly.

Later she saw him with Caroline. They were standing alone, looking at each other in a way which sent a jolt of alarm through Nicola. She recognised that flush on her sister's smooth cheek, recognised the excited brightness of Caroline's blue eyes. Turning her eyes to Lang, she tried to read the expression on his face, but had less success. Lang was using his grey eyes to tease Caroline's intimately—but then she had seen

him look at a lot of women that way and it didn't necessarily mean anything. Lang used his sex appeal ruthlessly when he found it useful. He was not necessarily
intending to start anything with Caroline.

'I'll drive you home whenever you're ready,' Andrew
offered at her side.

She turned back to him gratefully. 'Thank you. Do
you think we could leave now?'

They both glanced at Lang. 'Shall I ask him?' Andrew enquired without real enthusiasm. He knew
Nicola was here for Lang's benefit and they both
knew she would leave when Lang said she could.
Andrew wasn't keen on going over to break into that
tête-à-tête to find out.

'I'll see if Caroline is ready to leave,' Nicola said
lightly, and got a grateful smile from Andrew. If anyone
was going to put their head in the lion's den, he would
rather it wasn't him.

Caroline looked irritated when Nicola approached.
Lang turned his smiling glance at her and Nicola
politely asked if Caroline was ready to go. 'Andrew's
going to drive us home,' she added.

'Andrew can drive *you* home,' Lang told her. 'Whenever you like.'

Nicola looked at her sister. Caroline was smiling
again. The sensual glint of her blue eyes made Nicola
want to scream. She looked at Lang icily and he looked
even more amused.

'Goodnight,' he said in soft taunting tones.

'Don't bother to wait up for me,' Caroline murmured, her eyes lowered. 'I've got the key you gave me.'

'Yes,' said Nicola, knowing she was helpless. She couldn't make a scene and they both knew it.

As she walked away, Cary Lucci intervened, giving her his purring smile. She was so angry with Lang that she smiled back more warmly than she usually did.

'Your sister is very beautiful.' Cary sounded piqued and, looking into his eyes, Nicola realised that she was not the only one who had been watching Lang with Caroline that evening.

'Do you think so?' She flicked a look at him and away, frowning.

Cary saw her frown and moved closer. His hand touched her bare arm. 'Not as lovely as you, of course.'

The blatant, flattering lie almost made her laugh, but she controlled herself. She looked up at him again, opening her blue eyes wide.

'Thank you, Cary,' she breathed huskily.

She had never given Cary any reason to think she fancied him, but he forgot that. He was a vain young man, his own most ardent admirer. He looked pleased, moving even closer, so that she felt his thigh pressing against her.

'You know, you're wasted on Hyland, Nicola,' he told her. 'He doesn't appreciate you.'

How true, Nicola thought drily.

'A beautiful girl like you, with your brains, could get a much better offer. Wouldn't you like your own department? To be your own boss, instead of being at Hyland's beck and call all day? I'm sure you are ambitious, Nicola. You don't want to be a secretary all your life.'

He had tried all this stuff on her before. She could write the speech for him, although she was pretty sure the general drift of it had been sketched out by Lucci Senior.

'I don't,' she agreed, and Cary looked delighted. His hand was moving up and down her arm. The white teeth showed between his smiling lips.

'Why don't we have dinner tomorrow and talk about it?' he said softly.

She had no chance to answer. Lang was suddenly behind her, his clipped voice cool. 'I thought you were just leaving.'

Cary looked at him with frustrated annoyance, and then hurriedly switched his gaze back to her. He lit up with sudden inspiration. 'Let me drive you home, Nicola,' he beamed.

'Andrew's taking her,' Lang told him. His hand bit into her elbow, twisting her away from Cary, and she was marched away like a prisoner to where Andrew was standing with a worried expression. 'Get her home,' Lang told him brusquely.

Nicola met his grey eyes. They were steely. 'And I'll see you tomorrow,' Lang promised with menace. She watched him turn away towards Caroline again and desperately searched her mind for an excuse, any excuse, to part them.

Putting a hand to her forehead, she swayed and Andrew exclaimed in surprised alarm, 'Nicola, are you all right?'

She had her eyes closed. She slumped against him and Andrew held her, his arm supporting her back. Slowly Nicola began to slide downward. Andrew muttered something and then she was taken out of his grasp. She kept her eyes shut, making a muted moaning sound.

She felt herself lifted off the ground. Someone was carrying her. Through her closed lids she was aware when the bright lights gave way to darkness, the overheated warmth became a cool, fresh crispness. She knew who was carrying her and she knew he had taken her out of the hotel into the open air.

Lang put her in the back of his car. She lay back against the seat, keeping her eyes shut. He was holding her wrist—taking her pulse, she thought, and became oddly aware that her veins were thundering.

His hand slid over her forehead and her skin prickled with perspiration.

'She seems to have got a fever,' said Lang, sounding surprised. 'She's got a rapid pulse and a temperature.'

'What can it be?' Andrew asked, speaking softly. 'Should we get a doctor?'

'It's probably the last effects of that cold,' Lang decided. 'She should have stayed at home for a few days. She shouldn't have come out tonight.'

There was a silence. Andrew didn't say anything, but Lang sounded annoyed when he spoke next. 'I didn't know she was feeling off colour.' Andrew had clearly looked at him with criticism.

'She shouldn't go back alone to that flat,' said Andrew, sounding stern. 'She should have someone with her.'

There was a pause and then Caroline said: 'She won't be alone. I'll keep an eye on her.'

It was what Nicola wanted. She relaxed, fighting to keep a smile off her face. Andrew began to give Caroline instructions with a firm note in his voice. 'If her temperature rises you must get a doctor. It isn't like Nicola to faint.'

'No,' said Lang, and his voice came very close to Nicola's ear, 'it isn't like her at all.' She heard the sudden softness in his voice and almost opened her eyes because she could hear suspicion in the smooth tone. Lang was bending forward, his body close to her. She could hear him breathing. Nicola didn't register any reaction. She wouldn't feel safe until she had got Caroline back to the flat.

'You drive, Andy,' said Lang, suddenly sliding into the seat beside her. He closed the door and Nicola became inwardly alarmed. She heard Caroline getting into the front passenger seat and a moment later the engine burst into life.

As the car swept out into the street at a sharp angle, Nicola felt herself sliding sideways and tried to adjust her body. Lang moved closer and his hand slid under her back, his arm curving round her. She tried to resist the tug he gave her, but without betraying her complete awareness of what was happening she had no option but to let him pull her across the car. To her horror she found herself half on his lap, her head against his shirt.

His hand cradled her head, stroking her smooth hair. Nicola was torn between maintaining her pretence and pushing him away. She could hear the regular thud of his heart under her ear.

'Is she all right?' Caroline asked. Nicola heard the shift of her body in the passenger seat and guessed Caroline was turning to look at them. Caroline was taken aback by Nicola's faint. All their lives, it had been Caroline who needed looking after, Caroline who got all the attention. Nicola had always been the calm, self-possessed one of the two of them. Caroline wasn't sure she liked this shift in affairs, but she sounded worried too. 'It's so unlike her,' she said, half crossly, because Lang was holding Nicola in his arms and Caroline didn't care to see that.

'I think she'll live,' said Lang with a faint, suppressed amusement. Nicola felt his hand snake tighter round her waist and then, to her disbelief and fury, felt it moving just below her breast. She could feel his warm breath on her hair as he bent over her. Caroline was talking to Andrew, who answered her courteously.

Carefully, Nicola peered through her lashes. Lang was staring down at her, his face very close. He was amused. His lips twitched at the corners and his eyes glimmered at her in the shadows.

He knew she was pretending. He was doing all this deliberately. He knew she couldn't protest at the way he was handling her. What a devious, ruthless swine he was, she thought, staring at him. How typical of him to take advantage of the situation—and she should have worked out what he would do before she began her little diversion. She had hit on the scheme and acted on it without thinking ahead. She should have remembered that any move against Lang Hyland had to be thought out very carefully in advance. It was like a chess game; you had to probe your opponent's defences and counter-attacks before you risked a move.

The next second her whole body was thrown into shocked suspense as Lang deliberately slid his hand upwards over the soft swell of her breast.

Nicola's eyes flew open on a reflex action.

'Feeling better?' Lang asked as their eyes met. He asked it with soothing concern, his voice honeyed.

Nicola pulled herself up off his lap and sat upright, shivering. Caroline looked round at her. 'You are flushed, darling. Why didn't you say you felt ill?'

'She didn't want to spoil our evening, did you, Nicola?' Lang suggested sweetly.

She did not look at him. Keeping her eyes on Caroline, she touched her forehead with a weak gesture. 'I'm sorry, Caro, I do feel rather sick. I didn't feel quite so sick earlier.'

Andrew pulled up outside her flat. He hurried round to open the door and assist her, but Lang was there already, lifting her out as tenderly as though she were made of precious china. 'I'll carry her,' he said, and Nicola clutched at the side of the car.

'I can walk!'

'Nonsense,' he demurred. 'We can't have you fainting all over the place, can we?'

She would have retreated if she had had anywhere

to go. Lang's arm went round her waist and then he deftly lifted her with a hand under her knees. As he walked away Nicola looked grimly at him and he glanced down, grinning.

The mockery in his eyes made her colour mount higher. She felt odd as she looked away from him. If she hadn't known she was putting it on, she would have said she was feeling ill. Her symptoms were the same as those of illness. She knew she was flushed and trembling, that her bones had turned to water.

Lang carried her as though she was weightless. Caroline opened the front door of the flat and Lang effortlessly bore Nicola into the bedroom, laying her down on the bed. As he straightened his grey eyes slid over her before coming back to her face.

'You shouldn't have gone out tonight,' Caroline told her, standing at his side and staring at Nicola's flushed face.

'Don't scold,' Lang drawled. 'I think she's learned her lesson. Haven't you, Nicola?'

She met the flicking mockery of his gaze and didn't answer. Oh, yes, she thought, I've learnt my lesson. Give that man half an inch and he takes a mile. The physical intimacy he had been forcing on her during that ride home had been a punishment inflicted for ruining his plans for Caroline that night. Nicola swallowed. Whatever she did, she was going to have to make sure in future that she didn't give Lang Hyland a chance to do that to her again.

# CHAPTER FOUR

ON the Monday morning Nicole was delighted to discover when she got to the office that Lang had had an urgent summons to Edinburgh over the weekend. Andrew told her he would be away for several days. One of their current problems had suddenly needed Lang's personal presence and he had flown off on the Sunday afternoon. His absence gave Nicola a breathing space. Caroline wouldn't be seeing him, anyway.

She was seeing somebody, Nicola realised, when she got back to her flat that evening and found a note on the mantelpiece. Caroline would not be back until midnight, it informed her. It did not say where she was and Nicola held it, heaving a short sigh.

Caroline wasn't her problem any more, of course. She was a fully grown adult woman with a great deal more experience than Nicola herself, in fact, but that didn't help Nicola at that moment.

Caroline was hell bent on kicking over the traces and what could anyone do to stop her, short of tying her to a chair?

It did occur to her to suspect that Lang might have lied about going up to Scotland, but during the evening he rang from his Edinburgh hotel to find out if the Grettan report had been analysed yet. 'Ring me as soon as you get the results,' he added.

Nicola put down the receiver after talking to him and then, on an impulse, picked it up again and rang his hotel. When she asked the operator if he was staying there, she was told he was and her call was put through to his room. Nicola waited until she heard his deep brusque voice and then softly hung up.

He was there, all right, so where was Caroline and with whom? She watched television in a rather distracted fashion all evening, trying to concentrate, but her mind constantly wondering. She discovered who Caroline had been with at midnight. He brought her home and Nicola heard and recognised his voice with a grimace. Of course—Cary.

He came into the flat, looking around him with undisguised curiosity, and then smiled at her with that over-fluent charm. 'How are you now, Nicola? We were worried about you, my father and I. He told me to ask how you were. It was a shock when you fainted. Everyone was taken aback.'

'How kind,' said Nicola, smiling back. She was seated on her couch, casual in well-washed blue jeans and a loose white sweater. 'Caroline, why don't you make Cary a coffee? Would you like one, Cary?'

'I'd love one,' he said enthusiastically, sitting down beside her. Nicola flicked her hair back from her face and turned towards him, her chin on her hand to look into his eyes.

'You've never been to my flat before, have you? What do you think of my green horse?' she asked, gesturing to the ornament.

He looked at it, head to one side. 'Lovely,' he said

without any real interest. It was hand-made, hand-glazed, a piece of modern porcelain which she had bought in Stockholm on a trip with Lang the year before. Lang had held it in his hands, turning it slowly, smiling. He hadn't said anything, but she had seen the appreciation in his grey eyes as he watched her paying for it. The little horse stood about eight inches high and had a powerful, flowing grace of movement which the smooth bluey-green glaze completed. Cary looked back at her from it and she gave him a wide-eyed smile.

For all his good looks, there was something peculiarly empty about Cary, as though there was nothing at all behind his polished mask. He had neither morals nor scruples. One could say the same about Lang, yet she strangely hesitated to compare them. Whatever morals and scruples Lang had were his own, individual and self-determined. He was tough in business, but he wouldn't do anything he considered dishonest. He always kept his word, he honoured bargains. Cary Lucci was far less concerned with such rules. He did what seemed most profitable, honest or not, and he had no qualms about sticking to a bargain if it suited him to get out of it. He was weak, she decided, watching him as he talked about the musical comedy he had taken Caroline to see. Cary was a beautiful piece of flotsam, floating on a self-indulgent tide and happy to go wherever it took him.

For the moment he was concentrating his attentions on her because she was here and Caroline was in the kitchen, rather sulkily making the coffee. Cary had orders from his father to get close to Nicola, if he could. He had parental approval where Nicola was concerned and, no doubt, Caroline also seemed of possible use to the Lucci family. Cary didn't find it irksome to flirt with Nicola. She wasn't a sexy little blonde, like Caroline, but she had a cool, well-groomed look which Cary didn't find unattractive. Also, Cary was competitive and it irritated him that he had never got anywhere with Nicola in the past. It would boost his ego to seduce her if he could.

When Caroline joined them, she gave Nicola a smouldering glance. She had expected to find Nicola in bed asleep, obviously, and was now furious because Nicola was ruining her evening's entertainment. Tough, Nicola thought. It was Monday and there was another five days to go before she saw her maddening sister back on that train to David. She felt as though Caroline had been here for years, not two days.

'Did you enjoy the show?' Nicola asked her brightly.

'It was fun.' Caroline had taken the chair opposite and was aware that Cary was interestedly scrutinising her curved body as she lounged back, legs crossed, her smooth calves silken. 'I do miss London. There's so much to do.'

You can say that again, Nicola thought darkly. But you're not going to do it, darling. Not while I'm around to stop you. If Caroline's marriage broke up, Nicola knew she would never have another moment's peace until she got rid of her again.

'I must go,' Cary said regretfully a while later, glancing at his watch. Nicola walked with him to the door, to Caroline's fury, and smiled goodnight at him as he went.

'Will you get off my back?' Caroline exploded as Nicola came back into the room. 'I know what you're up to and I'm not putting up with it. I'm not your baby sister any more and I'm sick of your interference!'

'Have you rung David today?' Nicola enquired calmly, picking up the coffee cups without attempting to answer that outburst.

'No, I haven't, nor am I going to, because I'm sick of him, too,' Caroline snapped. 'I'm free of both of you and I'm going to enjoy myself if it kills me!'

Nicola carried the cups out to the kitchen and came back. 'What's gone wrong between you and David?' she asked anxiously, staring at her sister. 'I thought you were blissfully happy.'

'He's not the man I thought he was,' Caroline said bitterly. 'It's you he should have married, not me. I'm not perfect enough for him. I spend too much money and I actually want to enjoy myself occasionally. David doesn't want a woman, he wants a housekeeper, and if he thinks I'm getting fat to please him, he's wrong!'

Nicola tried to sort this out, her forehead wrinkled. 'Getting fat?' she probed, seizing on the least explicable of the statements.

'I'm not going around like a barrage balloon for months for anybody,' Caroline said, going to the door. 'And I hate babies—they cry all the time and they're sick.' She slammed into the bedroom and Nicola stared dazedly at where she had been.

She felt like the man who screamed Eureka in his

bath. So that was it! David wanted Caroline to have a baby and she was refusing. That was the reason behind this sudden reckless insistence on enjoying herself. Caroline wasn't ready for the responsibility of being a mother, so she was running away from David.

The realisation altered her whole view of the situation. Next morning she rang David from the office. He sounded politely wary as he talked. 'How's Caroline? I haven't heard a cheep out of her since she got to London. Enjoying herself, is she?' There was a distinct note of anger under his careful tone.

Nicola liked David. He was her saviour and probably she would have liked him even if he had been Dracula's best friend, but he was really a very nice man, quite apart from having saved her life. They had become friends early on in his relationship with Caroline and he knew that Nicola worried about her sister. She decided to attack him frankly.

'What's all this about a baby?'

David was silent for a moment. 'Been complaining to you, has she?' His voice had sharpened. 'Well, is it so odd? We've been married for two years. We have a nice house and I earn quite a good salary. How much longer is she going to wait? I'm thirty. I don't want to be a hundred before I'm a father.'

'She's petrified,' Nicola said bluntly.

'Why on earth should she be? You mean she's afraid of dying or something?' David sounded irritable now. 'My sister has three children and she's never shown any sign of being at the point of death.'

'Caroline isn't ready,' Nicola urged. 'David, you

know she isn't the maternal sort. Give her time.'

'Two years is time enough.'

'Can't you wait a while longer?'

'She's just being selfish. What you mean is, Caroline doesn't want to be burdened with kids and what I want to know is—will she ever want them? I'm not accepting a childless marriage, Nicky. I tell you frankly, I won't stand for it.'

'You'd rather lose her altogether?' Nicola said that gently and there was a long silence.

'Is that what she's threatening? To leave me for good?'

'She isn't threatening anything,' Nicola said quickly. 'I'm just giving you a little warning.'

'You wouldn't ring me to warn me if she wasn't up to something,' he deduced. A pause. 'What's she up to?' David's voice had taken on a hard, angry ring.

'Nothing,' said Nicola, crossing her fingers. 'But she's upset and I'm worried about her.'

David knew Caroline. 'I see,' he said grimly. And no doubt he did. 'Well, that's too bad, but if she prefers to walk out, that's up to her. I'm not going on with things the way they have been this past year. I'm sick to the back teeth with eating out and going to parties. I've had enough of parties and I'm not paying any more damn great bills for clothes, either. You can tell her that from me. Tell her to find someone with more money if that's all she thinks marriage is about!'

He hung up and Nicola flinched at the crash of the receiver. Well, she hadn't done much good there. The problem was deeper than she had imagined. Obviously, there had been rows for quite a while, and not just over the idea of a baby. Caroline was extravagant, she always had been. She bought on impulse when she was bored or miserable. And she didn't count the cost. Especially when someone else was paying.

David had come to the end of his tether, apparently. Nicola picked up her pencil and tapped her desk thoughtfully with it. Now what?

If Caroline did not go back to David, there was no doubt in Nicola's mind who would be stuck with her, at least for a long time. She could put up with a guest in her flat for a week, but she had no wish to have Caroline permanently in her hair. Caroline, in her experience, didn't worry about such minor matters as paying electricity bills or buying food. She would blithely expect Nicola to go on doing that for her. She wouldn't offer to help out with the bills and she wouldn't readily do any of the housework or shopping. Caroline was a beautiful parasite. At least David got something out of the bargain, but Nicola would just be landed with a lot of work, not to mention expense.

She sympathised with David, but Caroline was his problem, not hers. And he was going to get her back if Nicola knew anything about it.

That evening as she was leaving, Lang walked in and she looked at him with annoyance. Why hadn't he stayed safely in Scotland?

'I see you're delighted to see me,' he drawled, surveying her very unwelcoming expression.

'Problem solved?' she asked.

'Of course.' Lang wouldn't have left if it hadn't been, his voice informed her. He looked at his watch. 'You're late. Trouble?'

'No, no problems here,' she half sighed, because the biggest problem of her life was at home in the flat, not here at work.

'Then why haven't you gone?'

She didn't need to tell him. Andrew arrived, his camelhair overcoat open over his elegant dark suit, and gave an exclamation as he saw Lang. 'Hallo, we weren't expecting you back today.'

'Weren't you?' Lang turned his black head to run a thoughtful eye over Nicola's flame dress. She had changed ten minutes ago behind the locked door of her office because it would delay them too long if she went back to her flat. 'Going somewhere?' Lang asked.

Andrew nodded. 'That South African, Davidson, invited us to have dinner and visit that club you introduced him to.'

Lang's brows lifted and he looked at Nicola with amusement. 'Are you going to have a flutter?'

'I can't afford it,' she said demurely, smiling back at him.

'Don't we pay you enough?' he mocked. He glanced at Andrew. 'Get her some chips on expenses. We must keep Davidson happy.'

It was only a few hours later that it occurred to Nicola that Lang back meant Caroline in danger again. She was with Andrew and the short, bull-necked South African Davidson, in a Mayfair gambling club and with a pang of alarm she looked at them both and realised that she had no hope of detaching either of them from their obsessive interest in the tables.

Andrew wasn't gambling heavily; he was far too sensible. But he was watching Mr Davidson with avid fascination. The man's square brown hands moved firmly as he placed his chips on the table. When he lost, he shrugged; when he won, he looked impassive. I wouldn't like to gamble against him, Nicola thought, distracted. She imagined Lang at the table. He wouldn't show much, either, she realised. He had a poker player's face. He could act well enough to cloak any feelings. It was almost impossible to read him, at times, even when you knew him very well.

Nicola knew him very well. Sometimes she could read his mind as though his head was made of crystal. But even then, she often thought, her success rate was only as high as Lang allowed it to be—he often let her read his mind for his own reasons, which wasn't very comforting. She was never quite sure whether he was teasing her or not.

The glitter of the chandeliers overhead left the corners of the large room shrouded in dim shadow. The faces of the people at the table were cruelly illumined by that harsh light. She looked round at them all and shuddered. They watched the movements of the croupier with fixed avidity. Nicola found it distasteful to see such expressions on people's faces.

She was bored and worried about Caroline, but Andrew seemed oblivious to her restless movements. At last she touched his arm and he looked round, surprised. 'I've got a headache, Andrew. I must go home. Don't worry, I'll get a taxi.'

'I'll drive you,' he protested, but with reluctance, and when she told him to stay with their client he allowed himself to be persuaded. Davidson himself gave her an irritated look. She was a tiresome female, his eyes indicated. Smiling at them both, Nicola left, heaving a sigh of relief.

When she got to her flat she opened the door quietly. The flat was quiet and dark. Caroline was either in bed or out. Nicola crossed her fingers. Please, let Caroline be in bed.

She listened outside the bedroom door and heard nothing. Walking to the sitting-room, she opened the door and froze on the threshold in shock and rage.

The light was low. Caroline was on the couch and she was wearing a low-necked dress which was already half off. Lang's black head obscured her face for a second. He had been kissing her, but now he lifted his head and his eyes flicked over his shoulder.

Caroline gave a little shriek of dismay as she met Nicola's angry stare.

Dead white, Nicola snapped at Lang: 'You—get out of my flat!'

Caroline leapt up, dragging her dress over her shoulders and trying to zip it up with trembling fingers. 'Nicky,' she squeaked.

Nicola looked at her as if she had never seen her before and didn't answer. Her skin was cold and her stomach was cramped. Caroline put a hand to her mouth and ran past her out of the room, sobbing.

Lang slowly got up, running a hand through the

ruffled black hair. 'Your sister's a grown woman. Is it any of your business what she does and with whom?'

'Get out of my flat!'

His brows drew together. 'Don't talk to me like that.'

'I'll talk to you how I like in my own flat!'

'There's no need to shout,' Lang muttered, his frown deepening. 'Who set you up as guardian of her morals?'

'What Caroline does is her own business, but she's not doing it in my flat.'

Lang was shrugging into his jacket, buttoning his shirt, and she watched him deliberately with cold, contemptuous eyes.

He was looking back at her as if he had never seen her before, disbelief in his face. Nicola had been angry with him in the past, but she had cloaked it with smiles and a soft voice. Now she was looking at him in a way which brought a dark red colour creeping up his face.

'You're behaving like a schoolgirl,' he said brusquely.

'That's better than being a bastard like you,' she shot back icily. 'I don't give a damn what you do with anyone else, but you can keep your hands off my sister!' Having delivered herself of this with biting emphasis she turned to walk away.

'Don't turn your back on me!' Lang wrenched her round to face him again.

'I'll turn my back on you whenever I like! I've seen enough of you to last me a lifetime. I'm sick to my back teeth with having your discarded mistresses crying all over me, and Caroline isn't going to be one of them, if I can stop it.' She flicked a distasteful look at him. 'God knows what they see in you—I'd rather go to bed with a cobra!'

'Would you, indeed?' Lang's eyes were hard and narrow, rage glittering in them.

Instinctively she retreated as far as the grip of his compelling hand would let her. He stared at her fixedly.

'You listen to me, you puritanic little bitch,' he said through his teeth. 'You're not sitting in moral judgment on me, so you can stop it right here. What I do in my private life is my concern. I pay you to do what you're told, and that doesn't involve passing moral judgments on me. If you don't like my life style you can either close your eyes to it or you can get a new job.'

'Right,' Nicola said fiercely, 'I'll clear my desk to-morrow.'

His fingers bit into her and she winced at the strength he was exerting. Briefly he shook her, as though tempted to do more than that. 'That's entirely up to you,' he muttered as he released her and turned. He walked to the door at a stride and Nicola watched, feeling horribly sick.

She heard the front door slam and stood there, shaking. The room was wavering round her. She stared with darkened eyes at nothing.

It was a few moments before Caroline appeared. She was wrapped in a lace negligee edged with soft maribou fur. Through the lace her skin gleamed like pearl, but her face was very flushed.

Nicola slowly turned her head to stare at her blankly.

Caroline's face was tear-stained. 'You aren't going

to tell David?' she whimpered, choking back a sob.

Nicola didn't answer. She was fighting a sick hatred which was pouring up her body like lava. She looked at Caroline's full pink mouth and remembered the way Lang had been kissing it when she opened the door.

'I didn't mean——' Caroline sobbed, but what she didn't mean wasn't revealed, since she then put her hands over her face and broke down in open tears.

Nicola didn't move to comfort her. She watched Caroline immovably, her eyes filled with ice.

After a while Caroline wiped her wet eyes and peered at her, shaken because it was the first time in their lives that Nicola had remained aloof and unforgiving, whatever Caroline had done. Even when Nicola was at her wits' end because of some scrape which Caroline had got into, she hadn't been proof against her sister's tears. Caroline could see in Nicola's face that this time she had gone too far and she looked at her in silent pleading.

'How far had it gone?' Nicola dropped the words out like tinkling ice.

'He was only kissing me,' Caroline mumbled, biting her lip.

'Only! You're married. Had you forgotten?' Nicola's voice was piercingly angry.

'Nicky, you won't tell David?' Caroline implored, giving her the soft wide-eyed look she reserved for these occasions. Even with a tear-stained look she was lovely and she had traded on her looks all her life, but tonight she wasn't getting out of it that easily.

'David ought to be told,' Nicola said clearly.

Caroline's face revealed her disbelief and shock. Nicola had never betrayed her before. Caroline couldn't believe she would do it this time. Nicola could read her thoughts. Caroline was searching for some way of persuading her to forget what she had seen. She had come to London in a rebellious, affronted state of mind and determined while she was there to make some sort of gesture to her husband by flirting with other men, but Nicola sensed that Caroline was now stricken with guilt and worry. She might have intended what happened, but now that she had gone so far she was overcome with doubts. It was a typical pattern in Caroline's life. She had always been doing dangerous, silly things and then wildly regretting it.

The trouble was she was spoilt and selfish, over-indulged for years and without any self-imposed standards. She had wanted to have a good time, feel free and available again in admiring male company, but she didn't really want to lose David and now she was facing the distinct possibility and not liking it much.

'Nicky, you can't tell him, you can't be so mean,' she wailed.

'Why not? I rather fancy David,' Nicola said cruelly. 'If he divorces you he'll be looking for someone more suitable, and you said yourself that he should have married me, not you.'

Caroline gaped. Nicola could have laughed if she had been in a mood for laughter, Caroline looked so staggered and so horrified.

'You wouldn't,' she said incoherently. 'He wouldn't.'

Then, with a furious face, 'David loves me!'

'Does he?' Nicola smiled sweetly. 'He did, perhaps, but I wonder what he'll say when he knows what I found you doing tonight.'

'Oh!' Caroline exclaimed on a rising note. 'Oh, you bitch!'

She believed Nicola because it was what she would do herself if she wanted a man. She looked at Nicola with open-eyed jealous calculation. 'You meant to catch me out,' she said slowly. 'You planned this.'

Nicola looked at her incredulously.

'Yes,' Caroline went on, wiping a hand across her wet eyes, 'you probably planned the whole thing. You and that Hyland man—he wheedled his way in here tonight. I didn't suspect I was being set up.'

Nicola could hear the tiny wheels going round, the glib excuses coming out in readiness for any accusation from David. Caroline was busy creating excuses for herself, blaming Nicola as she had done in the past.

'I was crying,' Caroline said hysterically. She ran her fingers down her wet cheeks. 'Look at the tears. I was terrified!'

'So I noticed,' Nicola said drily because she was almost tempted to laugh except that she was still blazingly angry with both Caroline and Lang.

'I'm going home tomorrow,' Caroline announced, drawing her negligee around her with a haughty little gesture. 'And if you say one word to David you'll be sorry!'

Echoes of their childhood, Nicola thought. You'll be sorry, Caroline had always said, if Nicola threatened to reveal to their mother her latest piece of idiocy.

Caroline swept out and Nicola sat down on the couch, shivering. She felt very sick. Caroline was going back to David and that was good. But she had just given notice to Lang and that wasn't good. That made her feel like giving way to the sort of wailing tears Caroline had just inflicted on her.

She didn't, however. She sat there in the cold room in her coat and tried to work out what she would do, but in the end she went to bed and slept badly.

In the morning Caroline was up and packing by the time Nicola got up. Nicola glanced at her averted face with wry comprehension. Caroline would get over it in time, but for the moment there was no doubt but that Nicola was in the doghouse.

'I'm catching the ten o'clock train,' Caroline informed her formally. 'Thank you so much for having me to stay.'

'Have a good journey,' said Nicola.

She brushed her cheek against Caroline's cold one and went. She wanted to get to the office before Lang. She would have her desk cleared and be gone before he arrived.

She meant to ring David to warn him Caroline was coming and to beg him to go easy with her. If he trod warily he might make the situation work for him, but if he was clumsy he could make matters worse.

All thought of David's problems went out of her head when she got to the office and found Lang already there. Nicola paused briefly as she took in his presence, then walked into her office.

He was standing by the window. Turning, he surveyed her. She went to her desk and began getting things out of the drawers.

'Don't be so damned stupid,' Lang said suddenly.

She ignored him.

'You'll never get a job as good as this one,' he pointed out.

'Lucci will give me one,' said Nicola, and it was true. Lucci would leap at her. One phone call and she would be snapped up.

Lang couldn't deny that. Lucci would imagine he had got a bargain however much she demanded for her services. Nicola had a head full of Lang's secrets. She wouldn't part with any of them, but Lucci wouldn't know that. Nor, she thought, could Lang be sure.

'Have you been in touch with him?' he demanded.

She delicately shrugged her shoulders.

'What's he offered you?'

She closed the last drawer and picked up the bag into which she had placed all her possessions. Lang suddenly took it from her and tossed it aside. 'You don't really imagine I'm going to let you walk off to Lucci?'

'You told me to leave,' she pointed out with a queer painful flicker of satisfaction as she met his angry eyes.

He slid his hands into his pockets. His grey eyes shifted from her and he frowned. 'I was as mad as fire last night.' He paused and then muttered, 'I didn't mean it.'

'I did.'

She didn't want to go, it was true, but she knew that last night something had happened to her when she walked in and saw Caroline in his arms. She felt ill every time she remembered the way his black head had been bent over her sister, the way he had been kissing Caroline. Caroline's hands had been clasped in his hair, twining in it, her fingers pale among the black strands.

Nicola looked at him with unveiled hatred. 'I meant every word.'

He stared back at her, his bones clenched under the smooth mask of his skin, his mouth tight. 'O.K., maybe I shouldn't have done it, but she was giving out signals like a lighthouse and I didn't see why I should ignore the obvious.'

'You wouldn't,' Nicola muttered contemptuously.

'Good God, what century do you think this is?'

'You knew she was married!'

'So did she,' Lang bit out. 'If she had no scruples about that, why should I?'

'Because her scruples are her own affair—you're responsible for your own.'

Colour flowed up his face. 'All right, I've admitted that maybe I shouldn't have done it.'

'Maybe?' She used a scathing tone which hit its target. Lang stiffened and looked at her as if he wanted to hit her.

'Stop talking to me in that tone of voice!'

'I no longer work for you, Mr Hyland. I can use any tone of voice I choose.' She turned to pick up her bag and Lang wrenched her back to face him, his hand gripping her arm so agonisingly that she gave an angry cry.

'You're hurting! Get your hands off me!'

He did not let her go but his hand slackened slightly. He bent towards her, speaking coaxingly, his voice low. 'Nicky, this is ridiculous. You can't walk out on me just because I kissed your sister.'

She didn't answer, her face averted.

'Be reasonable,' Lang muttered. He took a breath and added roughly: 'Very well—I don't want to lose you. Does that satisfy you?'

'No,' said Nicola, turning her head to meet his eyes in a cold stare. 'I don't want to work for you any more.'

He looked taken aback, his brows meeting. 'For heaven's sake, anyone would think I'd committed some crime! You can't mean it.' He looked at her hesitantly, 'What am I paying you? I'll raise it.'

'It isn't a question of money.' She leaned over and picked up a typed sheet from her desk. 'This is my daily schedule. Whoever takes my place only has to follow it step by step.'

'Nicky!' Lang's voice was harsh and angry. 'Don't!'

'I think I've got everything,' she said absently. The row of plants caught her eye. 'Oh, the plants have to be watered twice a week.'

'Damn the plants,' Lang burst out, 'and damn you!'

He pushed her away and strode to his door. It slammed and the glass shivered. I'll never hear him do that again, Nicola thought. What a stupid thing to miss.

She could hear him talking on the phone, his voice

harsh and brusque. Picking up her bag of belongings, she took a final look round. On an afterthought she went over to water her precious plants. She wished she could take them with her, but that was impossible. She could never carry them all. On an impulse she chose her favourite, a deep pink geranium, and wrapped it in paper so that she could transport it without difficulty.

When she turned to go, Andrew stood in the door looking worried and puzzled. 'What's going on? Lang just rang me to say you were leaving.'

'I am,' she said calmly.

'But why? What's happened?'

His serious face was the last straw. Nicola put down her plant and burst into tears. Andrew exclaimed and came over to her, putting his arms round her.

'What's he done to you?' he demanded, and she almost told him, but she was luckily crying too hard and instead she burrowed into his shoulder and clung like a baby.

Andrew rocked her, his hand over her dark head. 'Nicky,' he murmured into her hair a moment later. 'Nicky, don't cry like that.'

She was subsiding already, the flood of tears relieving something of the anguish inside her. She lay in Andrew's arms, grateful for his comforting strength.

'Now, what's happened?' he asked gently.

'Lang and I had a row,' Nicola muttered.

'What about?'

She hesitated, biting her lip. She couldn't tell him. After a pause she said huskily. 'I would rather not tell you, but I couldn't work for him again.'

'I see,' Andrew said deeply, his voice oddly angry.

'I must go,' said Nicola, hiccuping a sob.

Andrew restrained her, his face bent towards her. 'Will you come and work for me instead?'

Nicola stared. 'But Tricia——' she began, and Andrew smiled at her.

'We can sort Tricia out—I'll shift her into running the typing pool next month. Mrs Lockwood is leaving, remember? I was going to move Janice up, but Tricia can do that instead.

'She might object,' Nicola said.

Andrew shook his head. 'She'll be getting a rise. Why should she object?'

Nicola was tempted. She looked at Lang's closed door, biting her lip. 'I don't know.' She would have to see him if she stayed. She didn't know if she could do that.

'You'll have the same salary,' Andrew told her.

Nicola laughed. 'No rise for me?'

'All right,' Andrew said at once. 'How much do you want?'

Nicola suddenly looked from his serious face to Lang's door. 'Did he tell you to offer me that job?'

She caught the expression on Andrew's face before he said hurriedly, 'Of course not.' Andrew made a very poor liar. His ears went red.

She looked down at her pink geranium, considering the small starlike flowers.

'You are a darling, Andrew,' she said suddenly, looking up at him with a quivering smile.

Andrew looked surprised, then pleased. He bent towards her and Nicola slid her arms round his neck as she met his searching lips. Andrew's hands pressed along her back and she yielded to them, letting him draw her closer.

Andrew had kissed her once or twice before, but it was different, this time. Her mouth parted softly and she let him deepen the kiss without resisting.

The room was silent as Andrew's kiss became harder, more demanding. Nicola found it rather pleasant to be kissed like that. She felt small and weak in his arms, leaning against him as he held her. She had been under so much strain over the past few days that she enjoyed relaxing and letting the whole burden of her life slide off while Andrew's hands caressed her and his mouth pressed over hers.

The door behind them opened and Andrew slowly lifted his head. Nicola didn't look round. She was looking at Andrew's flushed, excited face. Dreamily, he said: 'She's staying,' and there was triumph in his eyes.

The door closed without a word.

Andrew looked down at her, still smiling. 'Why haven't I done that before?' he asked her, and Nicola laughed softly.

'I don't know. Why haven't you?'

'I'm a bit slow,' Andrew confessed, grinning. He looked at her mouth. 'But once I get an idea, I stick to it like glue.'

Nicola lifted her face and Andrew began to kiss her again.

# CHAPTER FIVE

ON the first day of June, the skies opened and rain poured down as though it would never stop. The gutters ran with it, gurgling and splashing. Great lakes lay along the low-lying roads near the river and parts of Chiswick were flooded, which didn't surprise the residents much as it happened far too often. Nicola was dripping by the time she reached the office. Her hair was clinging wetly to her face and her coat was saturated, although she had carried an umbrella.

When Andrew arrived, he was bone dry, having driven in his car which he parked in the underground car park beneath the office block. Andrew, like Lang, only had to walk under cover to his car in the mornings and from it when he had parked it.

'Wimbledon weather,' Nicola told him wryly as he smiled good morning to her from the door.

He was as smoothly polished as ever, his hair brushed until it shone, his suit looking brand-new but his usual sunny smile was absent.

'Something wrong?' she asked, surveying him.

He glanced furtively over his shoulder and closed the door. 'Trouble,' he whispered.

'What sort of trouble?'

'Lang,' he muttered, and their eyes met in rueful comprehension.

She had been working for him for two months. Andrew was, as Tricia had always said, a lamb to work for, and Nicola could do the job standing on her head. Everything had gone beautifully.

Except that a succession of girls had passed through Lang's office since Nicola had left and Lang's temper had become volcanic. He took it out on Andrew. He did not often come into Andrew's office and Nicola had scarcely seen him since she walked out on him, but she heard him. The whole office heard him. The girls in the typing pool cowered as he walked past. They prayed he wouldn't ask one of them to work for him. There had been a time when some of them would have jumped at the chance—Lang was a very attractive man. But over the past weeks his frown had become permanent and the deep, curt tones could be heard from one end of the building to the other.

'What's wrong now?' she asked Andrew.

'What's her name, the one with the curls, walked out last night,' he confessed. 'Apparently Lang threw a dictionary at her and said if she hadn't learnt to spell by next week he'd force it down her throat.'

'Charming,' said Nicola, smiling.

'He blames me,' Andrew complained.

'You?' Nicola stared.

'He's taking the view that I stole you from him.'

'That's ridiculous. Didn't you tell him so?'

Andrew didn't answer because, of course, he hadn't done anything of the kind.

'I'll tell him,' said Nicola. 'If he comes in here,'

she added, because she wasn't going anywhere near Lang if she could help it.

'He told me to find him a new secretary,' Andrew told her, looking at her with appealing eyes. 'Nicola, could you?'

She smiled reassuringly, 'I'll do my best,' and picked up the phone. The agency were terse as soon as they recognised her voice. They had already heard from the last girl and they weren't keen on sending another lamb to the slaughter. The pay was very good, but Lang was being impossible. He had never been this bad in the past. Even before Nicola, the secretaries had stayed months rather than days. At times she almost got the impression Lang was doing it deliberately.

At last the agency promised to see what they could do, their tone distinctly unenthusiastic.

Nicola rang off and turned back to her own work. It was routine stuff and she knew perfectly well that she missed the extra dimension which her job with Lang had offered her. She had had far more to do there, but at least she had never been bored. Andrew was a darling and he never raised his voice, but Nicola was bored. It was all too easy and she was missing the adrenalin which working with Lang could produce.

Andrew had a lunch date with an architect from Gloucester and Nicola was just getting up to wander off to have her own lunch when the door opened. She knew before she saw him because at once her whole metabolism quickened. She felt fiercely alive as she

looked across the office, but forced herself to look
blankly polite.

'Andrew isn't here, Mr Hyland. He's at lunch.'

Lang closed the door and leant on it, staring at her.
Taller than ever, she thought, staring back. How does
he manage to look so aggressively vital? What does he
eat? It must be good stuff.

'Has he found me another secretary?' Lang had
folded his arms casually, blocking her exit, so she
stood there and nodded calmly at him.

'I hope so. I've spoken to the agency. They'll look
through their books.'

'Can't we try another agency? One that doesn't
specialise in mental cripples?'

'If you prefer another agency, Mr Hyland, by all
means try one.' She looked pointedly at his wide shoulders. 'I must go to lunch now. Excuse me.'

He didn't move. 'Happy with Andrew, are you?'
His mouth twisted as he asked that, and Nicola met his
eyes coolly.

'Very.'

He unfolded his arms, but only to push his hands
into his pockets. His eyes dropped and he studied his
black shoes with apparent fascination. She saw a faint,
hard flush creep into his face.

'You wouldn't like to come back? We could re-
title your job, call you my personal assistant. Give you
a higher salary.' He still wasn't looking at her. She read
the rigidity of his features with understanding. Lang
hated being put in the position of begging.

'I'm sorry——' she began, and he interrupted with a

furious snarl, reacting before she had finished because
he knew from her voice that she was going to refuse.

'Damn you, I'm not crawling on my knees to get you
back!'

'I didn't ask you to,' Nicola retorted, flaring up in an
anger which made her fingers curl with the desire to
hit him.

His eyes flashed at her. For a second she saw violence
seething in them, then he rapidly lowered his lids and
she watched him dragging a mimicry of a smile into
his face.

'Stop punishing me, Nicky.' He looked up again and
the grey eyes stared into her own. 'I can't find anything.
The whole office is in chaos. I can't work with any of
the girls that damned agency keep sending me.'

'Are you trying?'

She caught a flicker of something in his face. He
glanced aside and the black lashes drooped to hide his
eyes. 'You know I'm not the most patient man in the
world.' He looked at her through his lashes and gave
her a smile which was supposed to send her reeling.
'I'm used to you. We work well together, you must
admit that. Andrew can work with anyone, but I need
you.'

Drily, she said: 'Oddly enough, Mr Hyland, it is
what I need that matters to me.'

'O.K., what do you need?' he asked quickly. 'I told
you to name your own terms. I can't go on like this—
I can't even leave the office for a few days because I
can't risk leaving any of those pinbrained girls in
charge of it.'

Nicola considered him frankly, her face wry. She knew perfectly well it was what she wanted. She missed him, ludicrous though it sounded. She had walked out because at that moment she had been too angry to want to see him, but she had regretted it ever since.

Lang saw the indecision in her face and quickly he pressed his advantage. 'Have lunch with me, and we'll discuss it in a civilised fashion,' he proposed, turning his charm full on with a smile that altered his whole face.

You devious, unscrupulous swine, she thought, watching the smile in his grey eyes. Do you really think I can't see through all that phoney charm? Don't give me that sideways look or use your voice to wheedle me, because I know you. She preferred his tough, clipped voice to the one he was using on her now, and she had no intention of letting the smiling flicker of his grey eyes reach her.

All the same, she wanted to go back to him, so she shrugged and let him guide her out to the lift. She had watched him turn his charm on for clients so often in the past, but now it was being directed full at her, and although she had no intention of being manipulated by it, she knew that it was a strong indication of how badly Lang missed her and wanted her back.

He was doing it in style. Lunch at one of London's most famous restaurants, the Edwardian plush and gilt a soothing background, the food beautifully presented and the wine a first-class vintage. Lang was sparing no expense.

'You've made yourself indispensible to me,' he told her as he refilled her glass, smiling at her. 'I hadn't even realised how much I relied on you.'

Nicola fingered her glass, her eyes down. Only the best butter, she thought, and lavishly applied. 'Couldn't you trust them to send your red roses for you?' she asked drily.

He laughed. 'The occasion didn't arise.'

She looked up, surprised. 'Oh?'

He gave her a glinting smile. 'I've been kept too busy while you've been sulking in your tent.' He turned and beckoned the waiter to ask for another bottle and while his eyes were elsewhere Nicola looked at him. He was wearing an expensively tailored dark suit and, beneath the close-fitting waistcoat, a blue shirt with a navy-blue tie. The twist of his body as he turned to the waiter kept her eyes riveted. He looked round and she looked down again.

'What about you?' he asked, brushing back a thick black strand of hair from his forehead. 'Still dating Andrew?'

'He hasn't mentioned it?'

Lang's eyes met hers and she tried to read their expression and failed. 'Andrew is keeping his own counsel on the subject,' he drawled.

'Perhaps he thinks it's none of your business.'

'Sarcasm?' He lifted his eyebrows, laughing softly. 'Perhaps he does, but he's wrong.'

Nicola didn't answer, but the cool swoop of her fine brows answered for her. Lang watched her thoughtfully.

'You're far too dangerous for Andrew to cope with,' he observed.

Her pulses thudded. 'Dangerous? What on earth do you mean?'

'You've got marriage or nothing written all over you,' Lang told her drily.

A faint flush came into her cheeks. Lang watched, smiling. 'I'm right, aren't I?'

She looked into his wry eyes. 'Yes.'

'Pity,' he said, watching her colour deepen. He leaned back in his chair, his eyes on the table now. 'Marriage as a social institution is all very well, but it's only for men who've lost the energy to run.'

'What an interesting theory,' Nicola returned lightly to cover the different feelings coursing in her veins. 'Is it your own?'

He threw her an appreciative glance, recognising the sarcasm. 'Men are hunters by nature. They enjoy the chase. They don't want to get dragged off to the altar.'

Nicola gave him a sweet smile. 'Would you really describe Andrew as an unwilling victim?'

Lang smiled briefly. 'I'm sure he isn't, but what makes you think I'd accept you as my sister-in-law?'

'What makes you think you've got a choice?' she asked coolly.

Lang stared at her. 'Is that what this was all about? Were you showing me how much I rely on you to make me accept your relationship with Andrew?'

Nicola's smile went and she looked at him coolly.

'You know what it was about. It had nothing to do with Andrew.'

Lang didn't answer for a moment then he said impatiently, 'I wish I'd never set eyes on your damned sister. She's disrupted my life for the last two months.'

Nicola struggled not to feel. She tried to control the rapid rush of her pulses and the colour which came up in her face. She looked away, but she knew Lang was staring at her and when at last she looked back his eyes were sharp and narrowed and dangerously watchful.

He was far too clever not to start picking up signals if she wasn't careful. She had no intention of letting the stupid weakness she had for him grow. She had to be crazy even to consider going back to work for him.

He called the waiter over and they had coffee, talking lightly over it, not mentioning the subject which was in both their minds. It was only in the taxi on the way back to the office that Lang asked her again.

He was leaning back beside her, his long legs stretched out, his hands in his pockets. Nicola was glancing out at the shops they passed and her head was turned away when he spoke. She kept it that way while she listened.

'Will you come back?'

She fought with her own common sense, staring at the shop windows flashing past.

'Please,' said Lang in the deep curt tone which told her how it maddened him to have to beg.

She knew perfectly well that he had been deliberately indulging his temper to give himself an excuse for asking her to come back. He had torn those poor girls to ribbons without a shred of compunction and she shouldn't be insane enough to listen to him. She had got away from him—she shouldn't go back.

She turned her head. He watched her with an intent, unsmiling face.

There was something of the actor in him, she thought, watching him in her turn. He exaggerated his own character for his own reasons. Just as he had pretended to be seriously ill when all he had was a cold, so lately he had been turning into a snarling monster merely to demonstrate to her that she had to come back. If she didn't go back Lang would go right through the roof; his grey eyes warned her of that. Over the past two years she had become an essential part of his life and they both knew it. Of course, Lang could perfectly well cope with a new secretary. It was absurd to say he couldn't. But he didn't want to. He wanted things as they had been before she walked out. He wanted his office smoothly, quietly, efficiently run and he wanted to be able to fly off and know she could cope with any problem which came up in his absence.

Like most men, Lang had a passion for order. He had enough change and excitement in his private life. He did not want his working life upset.

'Well?' he asked brusquely, when she didn't answer.

Nicola sighed. 'I'll see what Andrew says.'

It was capitulation and they both knew it. Lang relaxed beside her, stretching his long body contentedly. He could handle Andrew. His brother had never said no to him in his life.

'Good,' he murmured, making no pretence that the matter was still in the balance. He gave her a sideways, glinting smile. 'You can bring your plants back this afternoon. I've missed the damned things. They brighten the office; the window looks bare without them.'

He had always said he hated them, that an office wasn't a damned garden and they cluttered up the place. But Nicola didn't remind him of that. He was saying it because he was intent on keeping her happy and while he was in this compliant mood she wasn't arguing with him.

Andrew looked glum when she told him. 'I thought you wouldn't work for him any more,' he said, and then took her breath away by adding flatly, 'What if he makes another pass?'

'Another pass?' Nicola repeated, staring at him. 'He didn't make a pass at me.'

'He didn't?' Andrew's blue eyes opened as wide as her own. 'But I thought that was why you walked out? That day you handed in your notice you gave me the idea Lang had offended you.'

'Not that way,' said Nicola sharply. 'He's never laid a finger on me.'

'Oh,' said Andrew, stupified. 'I thought he had.'

'No, he hadn't.'

'Then what had he done?' Andrew asked reasonably enough.

'I would rather not discuss it,' Nicola told him. 'But it was nothing to do with me.'

Andrew looked down at his desk and straightened his blotter. 'I thought he fancied you.'

Nicola hoped her face did not look as hot as it felt. 'No.'

Andrew looked at her in an odd way, his mouth wry. 'Well, of course, I did think it was strange.'

'What was strange?' she asked, bewildered.

'That you should slap Lang down and apparently prefer me,' Andrew said in a rueful voice.

Nicola looked closely at him. 'Was that why you started dating me?'

He flushed slightly. 'What?'

'Because you thought Lang was after me?' Nicola watched his eyes and read their shifting expressions. 'I see,' she said coolly.

'No,' Andrew said hurriedly, very flushed. 'I like you. I've always liked you.'

He had always liked her, but it was his belief that Lang wanted her that had made Andrew's mind turn to more interested pursuit of her. Andrew had rather enjoyed his success where Lang had, he believed, failed. What can you do with them? Nicola asked herself as she watched the porter carrying a tray of her plants back to her old office. Andrew was a very nice man, but he was as capable of competitive behaviour as his brother.

'You're not annoyed with me, are you, Nicky?' he had asked earlier, and she had looked at him with a wry smile and shaken her head. What was the point?

He acted instinctively; it wasn't a cold, well-thought-out campaign.

She arranged for Andrew to have a new secretary, a small, very pretty girl with eyes like brown velvet. Andrew accepted her happily enough, and, of course, Linda had no trouble with him. No one had ever had trouble with Andrew in his life.

Lang noticed the girl a week later when she came into the office. 'Not bad,' he observed to Nicola as Linda left, and got a tart look in response. Lang laughed at her expression, amused by the flash of her blue eyes.

The moment the office was back to normal, Lang's honeyed behaviour had reverted to type. As he had said, the office had been in chaos while she was absent. The girls who had come and gone had barely scratched the surface and she had a good deal to do before she could relax. Lang wasn't the only one to be glad she was back—everyone kept telling her how relieved they were. They had all suffered from Lang's black temper over the past weeks and his return to his usual impatient but bearable mood was welcomed by the whole staff. The first day he had put his head round her door and given her a quick, satisfied look. He hadn't said he was happy to see her, but she had heard him whistling as he returned to his own office.

Even his sister commented on her return. 'Thank heavens for that! Lang was becoming unbearable. Is he there?'

'I'm afraid not, Mrs Finister,' Nicola lied with Lang watching her and grinning. 'He's out.'

'Or under the desk,' said Monica, knowing him. 'The shares are down a point. What's he doing about it?'

'Don't worry about it,' Nicola said quickly. 'Just market fluctuation, that's all. They'll float up to-morrow.' It was a regular call. Monica kept her eyes firmly fixed on the share prices.

'I hope so.' Or I'll want to know the reason why, Nicola thought for her, recognising the tone. 'Any-way, that's not what I rang about. I want to talk to him about Toby.'

'Yes?' Nicola hedged. Toby was a distant relative of the family and Monica Finister had made herself his guardian angel years ago. He was a boy of about twenty who was putty in her capable hands. What her husband thought of it, Nicola did not know, nor did she care to guess. Possibly the busy Mr Finister seldom took time off his Harley Street practice to consider the question.

'Toby isn't happy with that stockbroker. I think he would do better in property.'

'I see.' Nicola looked at Lang and he raised his brows enquiringly. 'Well, as soon as he gets back I'll tell him,' she said.

'No,' Monica said quickly. 'Just tell him to come down here for the weekend, would you? I want to talk to him face to face. I know Lang's habit of ducking out in the middle of a conversation.'

'I'll tell him,' Nicola promised, hanging up.

'Tell me what?' Lang asked grimly.

She reported the conversation and he made a horrible face. 'That little twerp? He's not working in my office!'

Nicola did not answer that. Monica had a way of getting Lang to do things, however hard he protested. Lang knew it, too. He chewed on his lower lip, eyeing her.

'What are you doing this weekend?'

'Andrew's taking me sailing,' Nicola said quickly.

Distracted, Lang asked: 'Are you another of these boat fanatics?'

'I like sailing,' she said unrevealingly.

He shrugged that aside. 'Well, never mind, tell Andrew you can't go and come down to my sister's with me.'

'You take my breath away,' Nicola told him sarcastically. 'I'm prepared to be your buffer in this office but my weekends are my own.'

'You've met Toby,' he said.

Nicola had and her eyes were resigned as she met his frank stare.

'You don't want him around here all day any more than I do,' Lang insisted.

She moved to the door.

'Where are you going?' demanded Lang, standing up.

'To tell Andrew I can't come,' Nicola retorted, and he sat down again with a grin. If there was one person in this world who got under Lang's skin it was Monica, and he just did not dare go down to her house for a whole weekend alone. Monica was thick-skinned and determined. However loudly Lang roared it would do him no good. In a battle of wills, Monica always won.

'Don't leave me alone with her,' he commanded in the car going down to Sillory. 'And change the subject every time she mentions Toby.' He changed gear, frowning. 'If I were Joe, I'd have strangled that boy by now.'

'Maybe Mr Finister's grateful to him,' Nicola said, and Lang burst out laughing.

'You're absolutely right. Toby keeps her occupied. Monica without anything to keep her busy is quite a sight. I pity those kids of hers, she'll run their lives for them.'

Monica's children were all away at boarding school at the moment. Sillory was a large, elegantly proportioned house with a carefully maintained garden. There wasn't a weed in sight; they wouldn't dare grow in those flowerbeds, Nicola decided, looking round as she got out of the car. Monica wouldn't have it.

She followed Lang across the spacious, sunny hall and Monica looked round as they entered and gave Nicola a sharp, interested look.

'Hallo,' she said. 'I didn't invite you.'

Nicola felt her skin heating.

'No, I did,' Lang rapped back. 'Don't be so bloody rude, Monica.'

'I wasn't being rude,' she retorted. 'Merely frank. I'm glad to see you, Nicola, don't think I'm not, but I just don't remember inviting you. All the same, nice of you to come.' She turned her smile on Lang, her even white teeth showing between her lips. 'Now, I wonder why you saw fit to bring her.'

'Perhaps I thought a weekend in the country wouldn't do her any harm,' Lang evaded.

'Ha, ha,' retorted Monica. 'The day you start showing concern for your staff I'll start growing wings!'

'Which room can she have?' Lang demanded, ignoring that.

Monica shrugged. 'The one next to yours, I suppose.'

'I'll take her up,' said Lang, whisking Nicola off out of the room.

'Sorry about Monica's bad manners,' he muttered as they went up the stairs.

'I'm used to them,' Nicola said calmly. 'She's very like you.'

'Oh, thanks,' he said, looking offended.

'You have the same colouring and eyes.' Monica was quite attractive in an over-assertive fashion. She was slim and dressed well, her eyes were a cool grey and she could smile with as much charm as Lang when she decided it was worth the effort.

He showed her the room next to his own and left her, still rather offended. Nicola explored her new territory curiously. Monica had good taste. Her choice of colours blended well and the furniture was modern without being over-intrusive.

Nicola glanced into the small shower cubicle attached to the room and eventually decided to take a quick shower before she went down again. She had heard Lang wander off a few moments ago, but he had not knocked on her door so he wouldn't be afraid of spending a few moments alone with his sister. It was

Monica's continual water-dropping-on-a-stone techniques that Lang hated.

She stripped and stood under the lukewarm jet of water, turning with closed eyes to let it wash down her back. When she came out of the cubicle with her enormous white towel firmly anchored round her breasts, it was a shock to her to find Lang sitting on her bed.

Her colour rose sharply. How long had he been there? She glanced back at the cubicle, furious to realise that he could well have been watching her through the fluted smoky glass. She would not have heard him come in because the water had shut out all other sounds.

Turning, she found him staring at her, his eyes curious, wandering down her body as though he were making an itemised assessment.

'You should have knocked!' she accused.

'I did, but you didn't hear.' Lang looked up from her bare, damp legs to her flushed face. 'I told you that you were too thin. Do you skip meals?'

'What do you want?' Nicola demanded tersely.

'There's a question,' he drawled, grinning.

Her colour grew even more heated. 'Would you mind going? I want to get dressed.'

He rose and she backed. Lang laughed under his breath and that bothered her even more. She didn't like the bright gleam in his eyes.

'You shouldn't be in here,' Nicola muttered as he moved towards her.

She thought from the direction he was taking that he

was going to the door, but he gave a sudden swerve when he was level with her. She turned to evade him. His hands closed over her shoulders and pulled her round to face him. His fingers spread over the bare, smooth skin and Nicola glared up at him.

'Let me go! I'm not one of your blondes.'

He watched her mouth as she spoke and to her dismay she felt the flesh of her lips burning as though he had touched it. Her heart beat with a sudden, savage pulse.

Angrily she put her hands against his shoulders to push him away. 'Will you stop it? You're making me angry!'

The violence of her movement dislodged her towel. She gave a thick groan of dismay, grabbing for it, and Lang caught her wrists and held her, struggling bitterly, while the towel slid to the floor.

'Oh,' Nicola wailed. 'Oh!' She was speechless, her face scarlet.

Lang began to laugh and she glared at him in helpless, impotent rage. 'It isn't funny!'

His laughter stopped. His eyes flashed down her and took in every inch. 'No,' he said huskily, 'it isn't.'

There was a prolonged moment when they looked at each other. She couldn't stop shaking. Lang bent his head and his mouth closed fiercely over hers. Her hands curled. Lang released them, giving a deep murmur of satisfaction against her lips, then his arms slid round her to pull her close against his own body. She felt perspiration spring out all over her and her fingers gripped his shirt.

Her lips had parted, yielding mindlessly to the heated demand he was making. Her blood sang in her ears. A strange, burning ache began inside her and she struggled uselessly to pull herself free of the feverish vortex into which his caresses were dragging her. She could feel intensely the long fingers sliding up and down her back, the hard thigh forced against her own.

Her arms slid round his neck and she caressed his black head, her head dropping back under the onslaught of his mouth.

His lips left hers with reluctance. She opened her eyes dazedly and they looked at each other in a thick silence. Lang's skin was hot and taut, his grey eyes fierce with desire.

'Why didn't you let me see a long time ago? Didn't you know I fancied you? I thought you would kick my teeth in if I tried—you gave me that impression.'

The heated blood began to drain out of her. She bit down on her lower lip to stop herself shaking. Pulling out of his hands, she bent down and picked up her towel and Lang watched her intently, the incessant movement of his grey eyes over her body making her shake even more. She hurriedly wound the towel round her breasts and held it there, her head bent.

'I don't even want to talk about it,' she muttered.

'Don't retreat again behind that frozen face, Nicky,' Lang whispered huskily, moving close again.

She backed, bitterly angry with herself for having let him glimpse any response.

'I began to wonder when you walked in on me and Caroline,' Lang went on. 'You were so angry. It just had to be more than moral outrage.'

Humiliation made her feel sick. She had given herself away and there was no point in making loud protests now.

'I hated it when you walked out on me. I'm lost without you now, Nicky.' He was smiling and she hated the smile in his voice, she hated herself for trembling as she heard it. She spun on her heel and stood with her back to him.

'Would you get out of here?' she snapped.

'What are you frightened of?' he whispered, touching his lips to her shoulder. 'Okay, you want me. Is that so shocking? Why didn't you drop me a hint long ago? Didn't you think I fancied you?' He was smiling and his mouth kept brushing softly over her skin, making her heart close in pain. 'I do. I fancy you very much.' He took a short breath and his hands slid under her arms and closed over her breasts. 'I want you, Nicky. Let me teach you about love.'

For a few seconds Nicola stood there, frozen, then she thrust his hands down and swung to look at him icily. 'You don't know a thing about love! Anything you taught me wouldn't be worth knowing.'

The contempt in her voice banished his smile. His face hardened and reddened and he stared at her fixedly.

'Get out before I scream the place down,' Nicola told him bitingly.

She thought for a moment that he was going to say something, then he turned and walked out without a word.

# CHAPTER SIX

BLOOD had rushed up to her hairline. She was shaking from head to foot now that she was free to release her rigid control over herself. She stood there, her arms wrapped around her body, biting her lip.

She had known for a long time, but she had never let herself think about her own unwanted feelings because it was all so pointless. Him and his blondes, she thought bitterly.

Her mind was painfully, permanently occupied with pictures which flashed through her mind one after another. She had tried so hard not to feel anything towards him, but every time she saw him she couldn't help staring, drinking in every detail of his appearance. They all came rushing back. She put her hands over her eyes as though that might shut out the pictures, but they went on, under her trembling fingers.

Lang in his short dark blue robe, his legs bare, his smooth brown skin stretching over his collarbone as he leaned forward to get something; Lang in his shirt-sleeves in the office talking impatiently on the phone, tapping a pencil on his desk; Lang's powerful, long fingers as he rapidly sifted through the mail; the way his dark hair sprang from that peak on his forehead, the way the lines around his eyes deepened when he smiled.

Nicola had noticed every detail of his physical appearance. Not merely noticed—absorbed it, as though she were a sponge. The images had been stored in her memory, but now they were surging to the surface and she walked slowly to her bed and sat down on it, drowning in the sheer force of her own feelings.

It was a physical obsession. Giving it a name seemed to make it easier to admit to—after all, a physical obsession wasn't love.

What she mustn't do, what she had fought not to do, was give it a chance to grow. She mustn't feed it.

Her heart pounded, her skin pricked with fierce heat, as she remembered the way he had kissed her. She felt a terrible weakness in her body. Her mouth ached with the deep, erotic movements of his against it. As her towel slipped away Lang had pressed his body against hers, his long hard thigh tense, and she had been aching to surrender herself to the nagging obsessive need to know what it felt like to run her hands over him, to trace the smooth-skinned shoulder, let her hands move in an exploratory voyage down his back.

She wanted to do that the day he had deliberately stood there wearing nothing but a towel in his bedroom. She had tried to keep her eyes away from him, but they had kept going back because she was sick with a need to see him. Lang had been teasing her because he thought she was shy, because he thought it was making her blush to see a man half-naked. He hadn't suspected the truth. He couldn't have guessed how badly she had wanted to touch him.

It had grown on her slowly. At first, she had merely

found it exciting to work with him, then she had begun to feel alive only when Lang was with her. She hadn't realised for a long time what was happening to her. The physical obsession had rooted itself before she recognised it. She didn't even know when she had started staring at him with that deeply concentrated hunger.

She hadn't known what passion meant until too late. She knew now. It was this burning desire to know; to touch, experience his body as intimately as though it were her own.

She had tried to shrug her own feelings away, kill them with mockery, because it was so damned stupid to feel like that about him, of all men. But it had had its own painful existence under the cool surface of her matter-of-fact manner when Lang was with her. Her eyes, unbidden, had kept track of his every movement. Her skin tingled with reaction every time he touched her. Her heart turned over when she heard him speak. Out of his presence, she was only half alive.

She had tried to hide it from him because she knew what would happen if he discovered his power over her. Lang might prefer blondes, but even during her first weeks in his office she had not been unaware that he found her attractive. Her cool manner had kept him at a distance, but those grey eyes had made his awareness of her only too plain. Given any encouragement, he would have made a pass long ago. But Lang saw passion as the satisfaction of a passing fancy. She was all too well aware of what desire would mean to him.

Whatever it cost her, she wouldn't give in to this stupid, weak-kneed craving.

She dressed slowly and carefully in a simple, cream-coloured silk shift and made her way downstairs. Lang was with Monica in the drawing-room. She heard their voices as she reached the hall. Lang was trying to interrupt, but he was having little success. Monica, in full spate, was unstoppable.

'And he's very intelligent, you know, he could go far.'

'The further the better,' Lang muttered, and was ignored.

'All he needs is a chance. You had your chance, Lang. Why deny Toby his?'

'No, Monica,' Lang said. 'No, no, no. Let him dig roads or swim the Channel, but he isn't coming to work for me.' His voice took on a deep, savage satisfaction. 'And if he did, I swear to you I'd make his life a living hell!'

He pulled open the door and Nicola met his angry eyes. He strode past her without acknowledging her and she hovered on the threshold, not sure whether to go in or not.

'Come in,' Nicola heard, and then Monica peered at her through the open door. 'Don't just stand there like a refugee.'

Nicola reluctantly joined her and Monica pointed to a chair. 'Tea?' she asked, beginning to pour a cup without waiting for a reply. 'Lang's being very annoying. He needn't think he's heard the last of it.'

Her short dark hair curled round her face, but it

could not soften the square, aggressive lines of it, and her grey eyes glittered far too much like Lang's as she scowled.

'Selfish brute,' she muttered, savagely throwing lumps of sugar into Nicola's tea while Nicola watched and did not dare tell her she didn't take sugar. She was relieved when only three splashed in and Monica handed her the cup.

'How do you put up with him?' She lifted her eyes and stared at Nicola. 'Don't tell me you couldn't get an easier job! You seem a sensible girl. Why on earth do you stay with him?'

'The money's good,' Nicola said brightly.

Monica sniffed. 'Oh, well, if that's all that matters to you. Have you met Toby?'

Nicola had, and found him sickening. But she smiled and nodded.

'He's our cousin, but his side of the family have no money and he just can't seem to find a suitable position. People aren't helpful to a boy that looks like Toby. Jealousy,' Monica said on a loud note. 'Lang's jealous of him, of course. He's got a jealous streak a mile wide.'

The unlikeliness of Lang being jealous of the beautiful and limp-brained Toby made Nicola bite her lower lip.

'Who's Lang's latest?' Monica demanded, fixing her with a sharp stare.

'Latest?' Nicola looked dumb.

'Oh, come off it,' Monica snapped. She tossed her head and the pearls around her neck clattered. 'Is it still that Lois creature?'

'I haven't seen her lately,' Nicola compromised.

'Hmm,' Monica thought aloud. 'I hear you're seeing a lot of Andrew.'

Nicola met her eyes with a sweet smile and total silence.

'I'd have asked Andy down too, if I'd known you were coming, but if I have both of them at once, Lang uses Andy to keep me off his back.' Monica knew her brothers through and through. 'Lang has no sense of duty. He ought to want to do things for his family.'

'He runs the firm for them,' Nicola flared, becoming angry. 'If Andrew was running it, you'd soon notice the difference in the share prices!'

There was silence as she stopped dead, her face flushing. Monica looked at her, a glint in her eyes. 'I'm very well aware of that,' she said in an odd, soft voice. 'Interesting that you should think so, though.'

Nicola tried to speak and couldn't. Monica watched her and smiled like a well-fed tiger.

'Exactly,' she purred. 'You did say you stayed with Lang for the money, didn't you?'

Nicola felt very ill indeed under those shrewd, amused eyes.

'But you're right. Andy's a dear, but he'll never set the world on fire.'

Lang could, Nicola thought with a sinking heart. He could set fire to me, anyway. Any time he liked. She liked Andrew, she enjoyed his company. But he had never made her bones melt and her blood sing in her ears.

'Does Andy know?' Monica asked sweetly, and

Nicola was speechless as she met her eyes.

'Know what?' she hedged, and Monica laughed derisively.

'Obviously not. Poor Andy! Lang always gets what Andy wants.'

'Not me, he doesn't,' Nicola flared in reckless fury, her face fiercely flushed.

Monica eyed her for a long moment. 'Well, good luck to you, if you mean it. I said you were a sensible girl.'

Mr Finister arrived for dinner and sat talking to Lang in a smooth, faintly remote voice. He had a clever face which he kept under control all the time. His bedside manner made it impossible to know what he thought and his words were always carefully chosen in long pauses before he spoke.

Whenever Monica brought up the subject of Toby, both her husband and Lang ignored her and she had an irritated glitter in her eyes as they all rose from the table.

'Now, Lang——' she began, and Lang gave her a bland smile.

'Nicola hasn't seen your garden yet. I'll take her round, shall I, Joe?'

'Do,' Mr Finister agreed, smiling.

'It's dark,' Monica broke out crossly.

'There's a moon,' said Lang. 'Plenty of light to see by.'

As Lang guided Nicola towards the door, Monica said tartly: 'You won't forget she's Andy's girl, will you, Lang?'

He turned his face with a flash of icy grey eyes. 'I never forget anything, Monica,' he said with a deliberate threat in his voice.

They walked out into the moonlit, shadowy garden and Lang paused. His hand dropped from Nicola's arm. 'How the hell did she pick that up?' he muttered. 'Does she have radar equipment?'

Nicola didn't answer. She had betrayed it to Monica, but she wasn't going to let him know that.

'Monica sometimes makes me think she has second sight,' Lang groaned.

'She was just guessing,' Nicola said lightly.

'Think so?'

'What else?'

'Monica's guesses have an unlucky habit of being right and she knows it.'

'Maybe we could ask Andrew down tomorrow,' Nicola suggested.

There was a silence. She walked down the moon-washed path and heard the leaves softly whispering overhead. The scent of night-flowering stock wafted up to her from a great bed of it near the windows. Lang caught up with her suddenly and halted her, his hand on her arm.

'You can't marry him, Nicky,' he said in a deep, harsh voice.

'Why not?' She had control of her face now and could smile at him politely.

He didn't smile back. His eyes glittered in the moonlight. 'I couldn't let you—you must see that.'

'You couldn't let me?' She laughed shortly. 'You

couldn't stop me!'

'Don't pretend you don't know what I mean. You know it would be a recipe for disaster.'

'I think Andrew would make a wonderful husband.' She pulled away from his detaining hand and walked on quickly. Lang came after her at a stride.

'Not for you!'

'Aren't I good enough to marry into your family?' she asked tartly, giving him a furious look.

'Don't be stupid,' he said impatiently. 'That has nothing to do with it and you know it. If you married Andrew, sooner or later things would come to a head.'

'What are you talking about?' Nicola asked coldly; but she knew, and her heart winced as though pierced with pain.

'I couldn't accept you as my sister-in-law,' Lang said huskily. His face was sombre in the moonlight, shadowed and taut. 'It always bothered me to see you with him, but I'm not just being a dog in the manger, Nicky. If you were my sister-in-law and I saw you all the time, sooner or later I'd take you. I'd have to.'

Her face flooded with burning colour. 'It takes two, you know!' she retorted fiercely. 'Do you really think I'd let you?'

Lang's mouth twisted. 'You know you would,' he muttered, and her whole body jerked as though she had touched a live wire.

He moved abruptly to halt her and she leapt away, facing him, trembling.

Lang was very pale. His eyes stayed fixed on her face and he was breathing thickly.

'You conceited devil!' she broke out hoarsely and saw him laugh, but it was not real amusement in his face, it was a dry, comprehending admission.

'It won't help us if you lie about it,' he drawled, his lips crooked.

She gave up the attempt to pretend. 'I won't have an affair with you,' she whispered.

'I know,' Lang said flatly. 'You've made your position clear. Let me make mine clear, Nicky. I've absolutely no intention of getting married and I know you wouldn't consider anything else.' He took a deep, rough breath. 'Nicky, if I thought for a second that I'd stay faithful to you, I'd marry you, but I've never wanted the same woman for longer than a few months. I get bored and restless after a while. It's the way I'm made.'

She couldn't speak, although he paused to let her do so. Her throat was apparently filled with hot glass and every time she swallowed, it hurt.

Lang shifted his feet and pushed his hands into his pockets in that characteristic gesture of his, his black head bent as he stared at the ground. 'I want you very badly now, Nicky, but I've no faith in it lasting. If I married you, I'm afraid I know how it would end, and I won't do that to you.'

Nicola forced herself to answer that one. It hurt, but she swallowed some more of the burning glass and said drily: 'I don't recall asking you to marry me.'

Lang's head came up and the grey eyes smiled at her with a wry tenderness. 'You're quite something,

Nicky, do you know that? You're what Lois always used to call a classy lady.'

It made her laugh. 'Did she?'

'Oh, Lois had a very high opinion of you. You were polite to her and you listened to her problems.' His smile was gentle. The lines around his eyes and mouth carved themselves deeper into his flesh and Nicola watched and ached with pain. Lang paused, then said deliberately, 'Even though you must have hated her guts.'

That bit into her. She gave him a crooked smile and said: 'No, I think I was sorry for her. You see, I knew how it would end. I knew I'd be sending her red roses some day.'

Lang's lips moved in a self-mocking smile. 'You see? You know the score as well as I do.'

'Oh, I do,' Nicola retorted, 'I do indeed.' She was pleased with herself for sounding so calm when he was saying things that flayed her alive. She wanted to die of sheer humiliation. She had betrayed herself to him and Lang was forcing the admission of her feelings on her at every turn.

'I'm being honest, Nicky,' he said, and he had moved closer. His voice was low and husky, and she heard the timbre of it with alarm and wariness.

'Love doesn't last,' he said. 'At this moment I'd probably promise you the moon, but I can't honestly promise I'll still want you this time next year. All that moonlight and roses stuff is so much hot air.'

'Oh, let's be honest, by all means,' said Nicola.

Lang laughed under his breath. 'Oh, Nicky, you

make me laugh, and that's something none of my women have ever done before.'

'I'm not one of your women,' she retorted.

She saw the sweep of his black lashes as he looked at her. The grey eyes had a feverish gleam in them. 'Aren't you, Nicky?' His voice had a sudden, deep excitement.

She caught the hidden note of assurance in it and tensed. Lang was poised to move, watching her, and she realised he thought he had her. He was waiting for her to crack and then he'd touch her, and Lang imagined that would be that. He was giving her all this talk of honesty to prepare his way.

Oh, no, Lang; she thought. Not me. No red roses for me in three months' time.

Meeting his eyes she shook her head, smiling as coolly as she could. 'Sorry, Lang, no sale. You said you wanted honesty, so I'll be honest, too. You could turn me on if I let you, but I'm not going to let you, because I've no taste for red roses or diamonds and if I let you coax me into one of your three-monthly jags I'd hate myself. And I prefer to be able to face myself in the mornings when I look in the mirror.'

Lang wasn't giving up that easily. He was still smiling slightly and he took the step which brought him close to her again. His hand slid under her chin and lifted it. In the moonlight her face was pale and set, but Lang was staring at her mouth and didn't see the hardness of her eyes.

'You've no real idea what you're turning down, Nicky,' he whispered.

'Fantastic though you may be in bed, I'll pass,' she told him drily.

Lang laughed again. 'Let me show you,' he breathed, and although he was doing this deliberately there was an uneven note in his voice and as he drew her against him she felt the faint tremor in his body as it touched hers. Lang's mouth closed over hers. He framed her face in his hands and kissed her urgently. Nicola made herself stand still, not reacting. She kept her eyes wide open and she began reciting her favourite poem in her head, struggling to recall the lines. It kept her mind occupied and distracted her treacherous body. Lang felt her remoteness and his arms went round her. He kissed her with sensual pleading, his lips moving hungrily on hers.

It was a tremendous relief to her when he abandoned the attempt to make her respond. Slowly he lifted his head. His eyes were smouldering and his face was clenched in anger.

'No,' she said softly.

Lang's arms dropped from her.

'And if you ever try again I'll walk out of the office and I'll never come back,' Nicola went on calmly.

She saw his mouth straighten and his brows jerk together.

'You wouldn't want to have another procession of girls who can't spell, would you?'

He didn't answer, staring at her. The moon went in and she could no longer see his face, only the silver glimmer of his eyes.

'If you're right and love only lasts a few months, we

have no worries, do we? All we have to do is wait and time will solve the whole problem.'

She turned and walked away, and this time Lang didn't follow her. He stood there in the shadows and watched her walk towards the house. She heard Chopin drifting from Joe Finister's study, and Monica's loud voice competing with it. Joe was silent and who knew which he was listening to, his wife or the music?

# CHAPTER SEVEN

SHE was to be grateful to Joe Finister during the rest of that dreadful weekend. He gave her a chance to stay out of Lang's way by showing her his vast collection of gramophone records, many dating back to the earliest days of recording. They were deeply grooved and scratchy, but Joe was a dedicated collector who spared no expense to get what he wanted. 'I'm making a catalogue of them,' he said, sighing as Nicola exclaimed over his prize possessions, 'but it's taking me years.'

It was a wild inspiration that made her offer to help. Joe looked astonished and at first protested mildly, but he wasn't difficult to persuade and once they had started on the Sunday morning he was delighted to see how much faster he could work with help.

'You wouldn't like to come down every weekend?' he asked, half funny, half wistful.

Nicola laughed. 'Monica might object to that!'

'I object to having Toby here every time I turn round, but it makes no difference,' Joe said wryly. 'He never offers to help with my cataloguing, although he's always complaining that he doesn't have enough to do.'

While Nicola was engaged with Joe, Monica was pursuing Lang all over the house and garden. When the two in the study paused they could hear her yapping at Lang's heels like an aggressive terrier. They rarely heard Lang reply. Once Joe met Nicola's eyes and his held a distinct twinkle, but he tactfully didn't say a word.

Lang looked in once or twice, his dark face glowering, and Nicola met his stare with innocence, giving him a sweet smile. He made a few tart comments on what she was doing, but did not quite like to force her to leave Joe's side while Joe blandly watched him.

As she went down to dinner on the Sunday, though, Lang pounced on her. 'You deserted me,' he accused. 'Monica's been driving me cuckoo! I brought you down here to help me, not Joe.'

'Have you seen his old gramophones? Aren't they fascinating? I've never actually been able to touch one. I love the way they slowly wind down in the middle of a record—it's hilarious!'

'Hilarious,' Lang said morosely, looking at her as though he wanted to hit her. 'You're clever at it, aren't you, Nicky?'

'Clever at what?' She gave him her brightest smile and got a dark look in return.

'Punishment,' he said, striding past her into the drawing-room in a very rude way.

Joe rose as Nicola followed him and gave her a friendly smile. 'What a delightful dress, Nicky.'

'Thank you,' she said, smiling back. They had become friends over his gramophones. Joe was an enthusiast and came to life when he was talking about his pet subject. Nicola's fascination for his collection had conferred a new status on her in Joe's eyes.

Lang had helped himself to some whisky and turned to ask: 'What would you like, Nicky?' As he spoke his grey eyes appraised the slender lines of her body in the floating flame-red chiffon. He had seen it before, but he looked as if he was seeing it for the first time.

'Sherry, please,' she said, and he looked up to catch her glance. His face impassive, he turned away and poured her drink.

Joe talked to her as she sat down, still eager with excitement over the amount of cataloguing they had got through. 'No wonder Lang's keen to keep you! I wish my secretary was as quick-witted. You pick things up fast, I'll say that for you. You wouldn't like to take up a career in medicine, would you?' He laughed slightly as he said that and gave Lang a half-teasing look.

'No, she wouldn't,' Lang said shortly.

'Are the salaries good?' Nicola asked, and Lang shot her an irritated look.

'For you, yes,' said Joe, although he did not seriously imagine she would take him up on it, but Lang wasn't sure. He drank his whisky and turned the glass in his hand, staring at it.

'Where's Monica, for God's sake?' he asked harshly.

'What sort of salary range?' Nicola asked.

Joe began to tell her and she was quite interested because they weren't bad, although they didn't really compare with what she got at the moment. But it was an idea. She could remember it if she ever wanted to leave Lang.

Monica arrived in the middle of what her husband

was saying and listened with an interested, curious expression. Lang tried to shut Joe up by asking when they were going to eat. 'If we're going to eat,' he added disagreeably.

'You'll eat,' said Monica, raising her brows and eyeing him. 'Get me a drink, Lang, and stop prowling up and down.'

Joe had ignored them both and was painstakingly giving Nicola a clear idea of what a job with him would entail. 'Spelling,' he said. 'That's the chief stumbling block, I find. You'd be amazed how few girls can spell even simple words, and medicine is cluttered with difficult words.'

'What I can't spell I'd look up in a dictionary,' Nicola told him, certain that that would be no stumbling block to her.

'Ah, it's a question of shorthand, apparently' said Joe. 'They take down the wrong word in the first place.'

Lang was pouring himself another whisky. 'Stop trying to steal my secretary, Joe,' he said in a pretence of humour, but his smile was a mimicry of the word.

Nicola was thinking coolly. Lang was very angry and she realised that he was angry because he was scared she would walk out again. She had made her point pretty forcibly last time. Lang didn't want to go through that upheaval again. He was used to having his office run in that smooth, quiet way and he had missed her when she wasn't there. It was a strange sort of flattery to recognise that she was essential to him, but in a funny way it made her angrier.

When he drove her back to London she was quiet, watching the hedges flash past the car windows. Lang kept glancing at her remote face, his brows drawn.

'You're not planning to walk out on me again, are you, Nicky?' He gave her a coaxing, sideways smile. 'Did Joe's blandishments tempt you?'

'The salary wasn't high enough,' she said frankly.

Lang was silent, watching the road, his profile dark and unsmiling now. 'Or you might have accepted?'

'It's an idea,' she said lightly.

'You know I can't manage without you,' he told her wryly. 'Don't blackmail me, Nicky.'

'I'm not,' she said at once. 'I shan't leave unless you force me to.'

She did not need to expand on that statement; Lang's dry glance told her he got the point. For a while he didn't say a word, then as the car entered the great suburban spread of London he asked casually: 'What are you going to do about Andy?'

'I'm not going to do anything about Andrew.'

He threw her a harsh frown. 'You can't marry him. I've proved that, haven't I?'

'You mean you've proved that if I did marry him you'd have no scruples about trying to seduce me,' she agreed.

Lang moved restlessly in his seat, his hands tightening on the wheel. 'It isn't like that.'

'No? I'm sorry. Maybe I missed the point.'

He took the sarcasm with a grimace. 'You didn't miss anything—you never do. You're far too damned clever, Nicky. You know what I meant, however much you may pretend you don't.' He shot her a wry smile. 'I might start out by telling myself to keep my hands off you, but I've no faith in my ability to do that.'

'You've managed up until now,' she retorted tartly.

Lang stared at the road. 'I didn't know until now that you felt the same way.'

Nicola flushed vividly. After a long moment she said coolly, 'Well, it makes no odds. I've no intention of marrying Andrew—I never had. I don't love him and Andy doesn't love me. We're just good friends, as they say.'

Lang didn't say anything, but he began whistling a moment later and she felt like hitting him. The satisfied gleam in the grey eyes when she met them briefly later increased her annoyance. Lang imagined that his path had been cleared of all obstacles. He would have her there, in his office, day after day, and his working life would run as smooth as silk once more. She would stop dating his brother, too. Lang's complacent smile got under her skin as she considered it.

She could kick herself for having weakened even for a second. She should never have let him see he attracted her. She could see from the way the grey eyes flicked to her, a smile in them, and flicked away again, that extremely pleasant ideas were moving in his damned head.

He smiled and whistled all the way into London, a relaxed air of complete satisfaction in the way he leaned back in his seat, weaving through the other traffic, his black hair blowing back from his lean dark face.

He thought he had won hands down. Nicola might have threatened tacitly to leave if he pressed her, but Lang was in no hurry. Now that he knew he could get to her he would settle back to plan her seduction with the cool attention to detail he brought to his work.

She didn't need to use guesswork about that; she knew precisely how Lang thought. She had watched him for two years and there wasn't much about him she did not know like the back of her hand. Lang in operation was an object lesson in hard-headed patience, toughness and determination.

If he sends me any dark red roses I'll shred them into confetti and stuff them down his throat, she thought.

It was going to be a battle of wills. The only thing she could be sure about was that Lang wasn't going to give up, nor would he behave like a perfect gentleman.

She was going to need armour like steel-plating and a tongue like a razor. And, above all, patience. It was going to depend on who had the most patience; her or Lang.

As they drew up in the car park Lang turned, his fingers flicking her cheek lightly, and gave her a smile that infuriated her. 'You're very quiet. You aren't plotting against me, I hope?'

She looked at him derisively and amusement flickered in his eyes.

It was a couple of weeks before Andrew cottoned on to the fact that all his invitations were being politely turned down. He stood in her office with a glum expression and asked her point blank: 'What's wrong?'

She had thought out what she was going to say. She

could hardly turn round and answer frankly: 'I'm
nuts about your brother and so I can't go out with you
any more.' That had been true ever since she accepted
her first date with him.

So she had concocted a lie. 'I'm sorry,' she said.
'There's someone else.'

'Who?' Andrew asked, not unreasonably, but she
had been ready for that, too.

'You don't know him. He lives in a flat near me.'

'Oh,' said Andrew.

'I'm sorry,' she said again.

'What's his name?'

'James,' she said. 'James Fairfax. He's an architect.' He really existed, too, and he had taken Nicola
out twice, months ago. They had met at the launderette
and giggled over an old copy of *Punch*, discussing why
old copies of *Punch* were so much funnier than the
latest one off the news stands. James was cheerful and
not bad-looking in a disorganised fashion, but nothing
had happened between them which made their relationship deepen. He had asked her out a couple of
times since and she had evaded him. James had taken
the point and vanished. He was a useful excuse.

'Fairfax,' said Andrew, frowning. 'But I know him.'

Alarmed, Nicola forced a bright smile. 'Really?
What a small world! He's never mentioned it.'

'Oh, not personally,' admitted Andrew. 'But the
name.'

'Ah, yes,' said Nicola, hiding her relief. 'Well, of
course, you would.'

Andrew gave her a gloomy look. 'Well, that's that,

then,' he said, and Nicola nodded, looking as regret-
ful as seemed polite.

'It was fun, Andy.'

'Yes, well,' he said, shuffling his feet, not sure how
to make his exit. 'Any time you want a sail . . .'

'Thanks,' she said. 'I'll remember that.'

He kept his boat down at Burnham-on-Crouch and
got down most weekends in the summer. Andrew was
not a fanatic about it exactly, but he spent most of
his leisure time on water if he could.

Lang, of course, noticed that Andrew was suddenly
not in Nicola's room all the time and that they no
longer lunched together. He made no comment, but
his smile was two feet wide and Nicola observed it with
a strong desire to knock his front teeth out.

They were playing a leisurely game of hide-and-
seek now. Lang took every opportunity he could to
tantalise her. She pretended not to notice that he was
always bending over her while she typed or took dictation. When he deliberately scrutinised her figure
she looked blank. When he gave her that sideways,
charming smile she ignored it.

She didn't find it easy. Lang was using every weapon
he had, his voice huskily intimate when he bent over
her, his eyes inviting when he smiled at her. She was
tense every time he came near her, but she had had
months to learn how to disguise from him the effect
he could have on her, and she drew on those powers
of control now.

Lang played it very carefully for a long time, but
as the weeks went by and Nicky continued to keep him

at a distance, he began to get impatient. She knew when it happened. She was going on holiday at the end of July and during the week before that Lang became restlessly irritable, moving around her like a tiger around a tethered goat it can't quite reach; she could almost hear the lashing of his tail. It began to amuse her, and Lang read the smile in her eyes and his own hardened with fury.

He had expected her to be a push-over and when he met resistance he got annoyed.

On her last day at work before she left, he shot her a look from under his lashes before asking softly if she would have dinner with him.

'Sorry, I've got my packing to do,' she said sweetly.

She caught the flash of his eyes, then the phone rang and he moved to snatch it up, asking curtly: 'Yes? Who is it?'

Nicola had arranged for Tricia to take over while she was away. 'Who, me?' Tricia had wailed, and Nicola meant to have a few words with Lang, on the subjct of being kind to Tricia, before she left. She mentally made a note to remember it.

She watched him as he swivelled his chair, talking crisply, the lead from the telephone in his long, brown fingers. She really must stop looking at him, she thought with self-contempt. It was absurd—worse, it was dangerous. Because every time she looked, she was feeding the physical hunger she refused to satisfy.

He clapped the phone down and looked at her before she had time to look away. She saw the flash in his eyes as he caught her off guard.

Getting up, he moved to the metal filing cabinet behind her to get something. She heard his fingers swiftly clicking over files and then, before she knew he had moved, he was behind her and bending to whisper in her ear: 'I shall miss you while you're away.'

His mouth was moving close to her neck—too close. Nicola shifted and said calmly: 'Ah, yes, I wanted to talk to you about that.'

'Yes?' Lang asked, adjusting his body so that she couldn't slide out of the enforced proximity. He put his arms around her chair, his hands on the desk, enfolding her in a cage which didn't actually touch her. 'What *is* that perfume you wear?'

'I wear a lot of different ones,' she said calmly. 'I forget which one I put on this morning.' She hesitated a few seconds before going on, 'About Tricia.'

'Oh, God, not her!' Lang complained. 'Why do I always get landed with her when you're away?'

'Would you rather I got an agency girl?'

'What about that little thing with the big brown eyes?' he asked with a wicked intonation. 'I fancy her.'

A sliver of ice pierced Nicola's heart, but she smiled and said 'All right. I'll ask her to work in here and Tricia can go back to Andrew for a fortnight.'

Lang was watching her and the teasing smile had gone from his mouth. Although he probably did rather fancy Linda, he had been using her to make Nicola betray jealousy and he was annoyed because she hadn't.

'Are you going on holiday alone? Where are you going?'

'Spain,' she said, without answering the first question.

'Alone?' he pressed.

'No,' Nicola admitted. 'You will be patient with Linda, won't you? You won't throw things at her or shout if she spells things badly?'

'Who are you going away with?' Lang demanded, ignoring that.

'Friends,' she said. 'Linda isn't used to you, remember. Andrew will want her back in one piece.'

'What friends?'

'Nobody you know.'

'What friends do you have that I don't know?' He sounded as though that wasn't allowed. She had no right to have friends he didn't know.

Nicola turned her head to give him a wry glance and then wished she hadn't because it brought her dangerously close and at once she felt the sickening thud of her pulses and knew her colour had abruptly deepened. Lang's eyes observed it meticulously. He took a short, fierce breath and bent his head. Nicola had one second to move. She did, and Lang's mouth sought over her cheek before she pushed at his shoulder vigorously to halt him.

The telephone rang. He had to release her to answer it and as it was for him he stood talking by her desk, one hand in his pocket, jingling his change irritably.

Andrew came in to give him a sheaf of papers and lingered to wish Nicola an enjoyable holiday. She told him that Lang would rather have Linda than Tricia to work for him and Andrew looked belligerently at his brother's lean back. 'I'm used to Linda now,' he said. 'Why should I give up my secretary every time?'

Lang dropped the phone and turned to give him a little smile. 'It's only for two weeks, Andy. You can put up with it for two weeks, can't you?'

Andy argued for a moment, then shrugged resignation. As he was going he looked at Nicola and said: 'Oh, I bumped into Fairfax yesterday. Did he tell you? I mentioned you in passing and he said you were to ring him tonight.'

Nicola only just managed to look unconcerned about this, but Andrew's news had thrown her. What on earth had he said to James? And had James betrayed the fact that she had lied?

Andrew went off and Lang stared at her. 'Fairfax? Who's Fairfax?' he demanded.

'A friend,' she said, making a mental note to ring James as soon as she got home.

Lang picked up the sheaf of papers Andrew had brought and flicked over them. 'One of the friends you're going on holiday with?' he asked casually and on wild, stupid impulse, Nicola said, 'Yes.'

Lang didn't say a word. He turned and walked into his own office and closed the door with a quietness which surprised her.

When she was going that evening, he told her to have a good time in Spain, but his manner wasn't cordial. She left him sitting at his desk, his jacket off, his tie loose and a dark frown on his face.

When she got back to her flat she rang James, who roared down the phone at her: 'I nearly put my foot in it!'

'But you didn't?' she asked anxiously.

'By the skin of your teeth, no,' he admitted. 'Next time you use me as a convenience, let me know in advance, would you?'

'I'm sorry, James. It was a terrible thing to do, but . . .'

'Oh, I get the picture,' he said, laughing. 'Giving him the brush-off, were you? What's all this about going to Spain? Which part?'

She told him she was having a split fortnight, one week in Madrid and the other at a little seaside resort, and James said with amusement, 'I'll be in Spain next week—business, not pleasure, but I'll be in Madrid. Is that when you're there? Maybe we could eat paella together. You owe me something.'

'Why not?' she said, and gave him her hotel address. 'Ring me if you find time,' she said, which didn't commit either of them to anything.

'You think I won't, but I will,' James said threateningly, then laughed. 'I feel I've done you a good turn. When he started talking about you, I very nearly said I hadn't seen you for months. Lucky I've got my wits about me.'

'Very lucky,' she agreed. 'I'm very grateful.'

'Hold that thought,' said James. 'I'll claim my reward in Madrid.'

# CHAPTER EIGHT

HER friends were, in fact, neighbours who shared a flat in the same building as her own flat. They were a widely different pair—Joanne was small and giggly and changed boy-friends every month while Susan was sober and efficient and had had the same boy-friend for as long as Nicola had known her. He was in the Navy and had only been home twice in the previous year, but he wrote almost daily and Susan spent her evenings writing back. They were saving up to get married and Susan was buying all sorts of precious objects for her future home. She kept them wrapped in tissue paper in a cupboard and got them out to gloat over them when she was lonely. Very practical, she had made a list of the basic essentials she was going to need when she finally set up house with Terry, and she was ticking them off one by one as she managed to acquire them.

Joanne and Susan had been at school together. Their friendship was durable rather than close. Joanne was rarely in during the evening, and Susan saw as much of Nicola as she did of Joanne.

Their trip to Spain had been a plan they had made long ago. In the meantime, Joanne had changed her mind about six times, but she had always changed it back.

They spent the first days in Madrid in an orgy of sightseeing. Joanne was the first to lose interest in that, and for the usual reason. She had managed to pick up a boy, a Spanish one this time, whose name was Garcia and who rarely smiled but looked a good deal with liquid black eyes. Joanne deserted Nicola and Susan cheerfully. She said she was learning Spanish. 'I can guess the sort of vocabulary,' Nicola observed to Sue, who shrugged.

When James turned up Nicola tried to persuade Sue to join them on their dinner date, but Sue refused, saying she didn't mind at all being left alone for an evening.

'I told you I'd come,' said James as they ate paella by candlelight. The candles were purple and ridged with melted wax which turned them into strange shapes. By their smoky light, James looked quite elegant. He was wearing a suit, for a start, something he rarely did on principle. He was even wearing a tie, Nicola noticed, amused.

'So you did,' she nodded to him.

'So what was all that about with Hyland?'

'I'm sorry about it, but I needed an excuse.'

'Any time,' James smiled at her, pouring more rough red wine into her glass. 'I'd have said he was very eligible. Didn't fancy him?'

'He's very nice.'

'But?' James pushed some of his prawns around with his fork, staring at them. 'You do like to play your cards close to your chest, don't you?'

She smiled.

'I nearly said to him—join the club,' James told her wryly.

She flushed, understanding what he meant. He looked up and gave her a rueful grin. 'We ought to wear a special tie; men who didn't make it with Nicola Adney. We could have yearly functions. A dinner dance, maybe.'

James grinned to show he was still joking, but his eyes weren't quite so amused. 'But he wouldn't have thought it was funny, if I had. I got the feeling that either the wound was still too raw or he hadn't got a sense of humour.'

'How's your job?' Nicola asked, sipping her wine.

'Change of subject,' James accepted. 'Fine, thanks. Yours?'

'Fine.'

There was a silence. James stared at the smoky candle and said drily: 'We have got a lot to say to each other, haven't we?'

'Are you still unattached?' She realised as she asked that that it wasn't the most tactful question.

He leered at her teasingly. 'Is that a proposition? If so, consider it firmly accepted.'

'No girl in particular?' she asked, ignoring that.

'Any girl in general,' he admitted, smiling. 'I'm very easy to please.'

'I'll remember that if the subject ever arises,' she promised.

'Who took Hyland's place?' James asked, watching her.

She drank some more of her wine. 'This stuff could

take the paint off walls,' she smiled evasively.

'I'll take some back with me,' said James. 'I'm doing some redecorating in the flat.'

As the evening wore on, Nicola scarcely noticed that she was drinking more of the local wine than she would normally do, but she did feel that she and James were getting on much better. They laughed a good deal and said a lot of things about seeing each other more often when they were back in London. James was going back next day—his business had been done and he had left this date with her until the end of his trip. He said he would pick her up at Heathrow on her return and drive her back to her flat, and Nicola told him that was very kind and she would love it.

They walked for a while before going back to her hotel. The air was warm and slightly heavy. The wine had made her sleepy and she leaned on James as they walked, his arm going round her waist to support her.

'You're a bit tipsy,' he smiled, and she laughed up at him, making a face.

'Whose fault is that?'

'Don't blame me!'

'That wine,' Nicola sighed, shaking her head.

Outside her hotel, James slid his arm round her and kissed her. He wasn't in love with her, although he rather fancied her, and she felt sleepy and lazy, so she kissed him back quite enthusiastically. James felt this was a good sign. Encouraged, he held her closer and kissed her harder.

'Don't forget,' he said. 'I'll meet you at the airport the day you fly back.'

'I won't,' she promised, waving a hand in farewell, then went up to her hotel room and promptly fell into bed and deeply asleep, forgetting the whole thing.

At the end of that week they moved from Madrid to a small coastal resort where they put all thoughts of sightseeing out of their heads and just lay about on the beach, lazing in the sun like seals. The days were spent in sunbathing and swimming; the evenings were spent at the hotel dancing and dining. They had plenty of male company to choose from—Joanne fluttered from escort to escort every night. Nicola flirted lightly with a young man from the Midlands who kept calling the waiter *garçon*, to his evident fury. Susan wrote letters to Terry and sent him postcards by every post. She resisted all lures steadfastly, but appeared to be enjoying herself all the same.

Nicola's pale skin slowly deepened from a faint biscuit to a gleaming tan which she encouraged with lots of suntan oil and careful exposure on the crowded beach.

'Suits you,' Joanne said enviously. She had turned lobster pink and then peeled painfully before she began to acquire any sort of tan. 'Your skin takes the sun, doesn't it?'

'I want to *look* as if I've been in the sun,' Nicola explained.

'Well, you certainly do,' Joanne agreed.

It was only as they struggled through the Customs at Heathrow that Nicola remembered James's promise to meet her. She did not expect to see him. James had been slightly drunk and in any case their brief romance hadn't ever shown signs of becoming anything more.

She was taken aback to see him waving at her as she emerged to get her luggage. 'There you are,' he panted, darting past a clump of laughing people returning from the continent with tans. He stopped to look at her in interest. 'Good lord, you have taken the sun! Your skin's fantastic. You ought to be that colour all the time. You're usually a bit on the pallid side.'

'Thank you so much, James,' she mocked, smiling back. Joanne and Susan eyed him with faint recognition. They'd seen him around before but never met.

Nicola introduced him and James promptly offered them both a lift, too. They accepted eagerly, giving her a quick look to make sure she didn't mind if they joined her and James.

'Have a good time?' James asked.

Joanne and Susan walked on ahead and James brought Nicola's case along, his arm round her waist as they walked.

'Great,' she said. 'Good food, sea, sun—what more can one want of a holiday?'

'Girls,' James said gleefully, and she laughed.

A movement nearby caught her eye. She glanced across the great open concourse and saw Lang in a dark suit and carrying a coat over his arm. He was staring at her and James. She halted in surprise and James, still talking, halted, too, looking down at her. 'What's wrong?'

'Someone I know,' she said lamely, feeling her skin flush.

James looked round vaguely, frowning.

Lang was already striding away towards the exit. She saw a flight bag in his hand and realised he must also have been abroad somewhere. James stared after him and then looked down at her.

'Who is it?' he asked, grimacing. 'Strong competition, by the look of him. I've seen him before somewhere.'

'My boss,' said Nicola. 'Oh, we've lost the girls.'

'I can see Joanne's head,' James told her. 'They're waiting for us by the door.'

The subject of Lang was dropped and not reopened. James drove them all back to London, listening with amusement to their tales of fun and games at the seaside. 'I wish I'd known. I'd have come too,' he said. Most of the anecdotes had come from Joanne and her endless conquests. He glanced at Nicola. 'What about you? How many did you do to death with that smile of yours?'

She gave him a teasing smile. 'Hundreds.'

'I bet,' he said. 'More members for the club!'

'What club?' Joanne demanded, and Nicola began to say, 'Nothing,' but James deliberately expanded on his joke and they all laughed, but Nicola's laughter was forced. She wasn't really amused.

'I like it,' Joanne crowed.

When he left them at the door of the flat block, James held on to Nicola's hand and asked: 'When am I going to see you again?'

'Some time,' she answered absently. 'Give me a ring.' Her smile softened the evasive answer. 'And thanks for the lift. I really am grateful. It was sweet of you.'

'What's a fan club for?' he asked, releasing her.

She wished he hadn't come to the airport. She hadn't really expected it and it left her under an obligation to him, which may have been what he intended. James was lighthearted and he wasn't in love with her, but he fancied her and he was still hoping he might be able to talk her into bed some day.

When she went into work on the Monday morning she found Linda desperately trying to finish filing the great mound of paper she had not managed to deal with during the last fortnight. 'I'm sorry,' she wailed. 'Oh, am I glad you're back! They said he was frightful, but I thought they were exaggerating. He's so good-looking. I didn't believe he could be as bad as they said, but he's got a horrible temper, hasn't he? He wasn't so bad at first—then he got really nasty, and all over a little telephone call. How was I to know he hated his sister?'

Nicola listened and didn't smile but was tempted to. 'Never mind,' she soothed. 'Off you go back to Andy. I'll clear this lot away.'

Linda lingered, watching her. 'You are brown! Have a good holiday?'

'Fantastic,' Nicola said with enthusiasm as the door opened.

Linda vanished silently. Lang didn't seem to see her go. He was leaning on the door of his office, his eyes on Nicola, and she became conscious of a coldness in his face.

'Sorry to be back?' he asked, his lips twisting.

She turned to go on filing the documents she was holding. 'I'm not overjoyed to meet this sort of weather.' It was raining and although it was August London was grey and dismal and she hankered for the Spanish beaches and sunshine.

Lang didn't move or speak for a moment. 'You went away, I gather?' she asked politely.

'I had to go to Denmark. I was in Copenhagen for a couple of days. It was raining there, too.'

'Tough luck,' she said, turning to smile at him.

'You enjoyed yourself, I gather.'

'Very much. It was a relaxing fortnight.'

Lang watched her close the cabinet with a metallic clang. She glanced round and was taken aback by the way he was staring at her, his eyes icy.

'Was that Fairfax at the airport?' he asked suddenly, and she caught on with a rush to what was in his mind.

She had told him she was going away with James and he had seen them together at the airport. Lang was looking at her like a tiger whose goat has been eaten by someone else. For a second it was on her lips to say: don't be silly. Of course I haven't. Then she swallowed the words unspoken, as she realised she had been thrown a lifebelt.

Looking at him as brightly as she could, she said: 'Yes, that was James.'

'How long have you known him? You didn't tell me there was someone hanging around.' He sounded terse, accusing, but she pretended not to notice.

'Oh, James and I go way back,' she said casually.

Lang's eyes narrowed. 'Old friends, you mean?' He liked that, she saw. That suited him.

Shrugging, she said: 'We've been seeing each other for weeks.' She paused and added: 'Since I stopped dating Andrew.'

His frown returned. His eyes bored into her, searching her face.

'I decided to take your advice,' Nicola said lightly.

'Advice? My advice?' Lang had a harsh ring to his voice as he repeated the words.

'Yes,' she said as the telephone rang. Moving to answer it, she gave him a bright smile. 'When you need advice, always ask an expert.'

It was Monica. 'Oh, you're back,' she said.

Nicola almost said: sorry. Monica had only got through to Lang because she was away and her irritation was in her voice.

'Is he there?' she asked, and added drily, 'Don't tell me, he's out.'

'Not in yet,' Nicola expanded softly. 'When he does get in, I'll tell him you rang.'

'I'm sure you will,' Monica said tartly.

'Can I help you, in the meantime?' Nicola was bland and syrupy, but Monica wasn't fooled.

'You can tell me when the statements are going to be out.'

'Very soon,' Nicola soothed. 'They aren't due until the end of the month.'

'I'd like to get a peep before that,' said Monica, as if Nicola didn't know that.

'As soon as they come from the printer, you'll have

one,' Nicola promised, and rang off.

Lang had left the room. She heard him banging things. She had noticed before that when he was in a temper he became noisier, slamming doors and phones down, unable to find whatever he looked for and getting more furious as he searched.

'What have you done with my pen?' he demanded, materialising in the doorway. 'I can't find the damned thing.'

She didn't bother to point out that she had been away for a fortnight. When he lost anything she was always to blame.

She found his pen on his desk under a letter. He accepted it grimly.

'Are we going to do any work?' he demanded with his jaw aggressive.

Nicola forbore to comment. The morning passed in a permanent atmosphere of battle. Lang sniped and muttered and looked at her as if he could willingly slap her. Nicola smiled and spoke softly and pretended not to notice his mood.

He went off to lunch at one and Nicola strolled through the busy streets with the intention of skipping food and shopping for a birthday present for Joanne, whose birthday fell that week.

Peering into a jeweller's window she heard someone exclaim behind her and turned to see Cary Lucci. He admired her tan extravagantly and she thanked him with faint dryness. 'What are you hoping someone will buy you?' he asked with a glint in his dark eyes.

Straight-faced she said: 'The sapphire ring.'

He shot it a look and noted the price and smiled hurriedly. 'Lovely,' he said.

She felt mischievous. Fluttering her lashes at him, she said wistfully: 'Sapphires are my favourite stones.'

Not at that price, Cary's face said, but aloud he asked: 'Will you have lunch with me?'

'I would have loved to, but I've got a lot of shopping to do,' she evaded. 'Nice to see you, Cary.'

As she turned to go he caught her elbow and bent towards her, smiling with as much charm as he could muster. 'Is Lang taking you to the party tonight?'

'Party?' she repeated. Lang hadn't even mentioned a party. Her veins turned to ice as she contemplated what that must mean. He would be taking someone else. Who had he met while she was away? A blonde, she thought bitterly. A hundred to one, it's a blonde.

Cary caught the echo of chagrin in her voice and his smile widened. 'No? Then will you come with me, Nicky?'

'What party is it?' she asked blankly, fighting with a horrible desire to scream.

'Launching the redevelopment scheme,' he said. 'Our tender was accepted, remember? Lang accepted, I'm sure he did.'

Lang would have done. Their tender had been turned down because Lucci had cut the figures below that level which Lang thought profitable. Lang had been livid. 'He'll lose money on it,' he had said furiously, but he would go to the party and see what he could pick up about how Lucci planned to make his development plans pay.

Nicola had it on the tip of her tongue to refuse when on impulse she said: 'Thank you, I'd love to go with you.'

Cary beamed. 'Shall I pick you up at your flat?'

'Could you? What time?'

'Eight,' he said. 'We'll have a ball, Nicky.'

That's what you think, she told herself, as she walked away.

It wasn't until just before she left work that evening that Lang suddenly said: 'Oh, I forgot. There's a party tonight—Lucci showing off his prize again, the development at Ealing. You'd better come along.'

Nicola hesitated. She had been wrong; he wasn't taking anyone else. Lang looked at her sharply.

'Going somewhere else?'

She couldn't meet his eyes. He wasn't going to like it, but she could hardly back out now. 'Cary asked me,' she mumbled.

'What?' demanded Lang. 'What did you say?'

'Well, I didn't know.' She almost backed at his tone. 'You should have said something earlier.'

'Cary Lucci?' he said, as if he had never heard of Cary. 'Cary Lucci asked you to the party and you accepted?'

'You usually give me warning if I have to be there, so I assumed you wouldn't want me along with you.'

'Oh, you assumed that, did you?' She heard his long intake of breath and waited for the explosion. 'Since when did you think I'd approve of you going around with one of the Lucci family? No, don't answer that.' His voice was heavy with sarcasm. 'Let me guess. I'm

really getting it, aren't I? You have a genius for sticking knives in people's backs. I haven't worked with
you for two years without discovering that under that
quiet face of yours you can be damned lethal. I stepped
out of line and now I'm being taught to stay in my
place, am I?'

'I'm not sticking any knife in your back,' she protested, furious with the accusation.

'You knew I'd want you with me. When have I ever
gone to one of Lucci's parties alone?' He drew breath,
his voice becoming deeper and more angry. 'You knew
it would make me mad to see you there with Cary
Lucci, and that's what you want, isn't it? To drive
me out of my mind if you can.' His skin was a dark,
furious red and his eyes bit into her. 'You forget, I'm
used to your little campaigns. You and my sister have
a lot in common—you just go about it in a different
way. Monica talks my head off. You're clever with it.
You drive me out of my mind altogether.'

Nicola was alarmed by the violence in his face. Hurriedly she gave him a sweet, coaxing smile. 'Maybe I
could get hold of Cary—tell him I'd forgotten I'd promised to go with you.'

'Don't turn the honey on for me!' he bellowed. 'Go
with him. I don't damned well care.' He went out of
the room like a bullet from a gun, but as she was beginning to relax, shot back to snarl: 'Just don't think
I'll forget it. And watch yourself with him, because I'll
be watching too!'

He flung out again, slamming the door, and she
stared at in stupefaction. She had never been indis-

creet or disloyal in the two years she had worked for him and he had no right to suggest she would be now. Her eyes flared with anger. One day, she thought, one day, Lang, I'll tip you out of a window!

Cary picked her up dead on eight and looked at her with genuine appreciation as he greeted her. His admiration was normally slightly artificial, but not tonight. The little black dress, which made her look invisible when her skin was pale, looked quite different on her now that she was a glowing, smooth gold. She knew the tan wouldn't last. It never did. But for the moment she looked and felt fantastic. She was wearing a wide scarlet band of braid in her hair—she had bought it in Spain to match some beach mules, but it came in handy to give her black dress a touch of colour. Her lipstick matched it, the glistening colour very vivid against her tanned skin. She hadn't bothered to do more than dust her skin lightly with powder, but she was wearing a glittery eye make-up which made her eyes look bigger and bluer.

Confident that she looked good, she smiled at Cary. You couldn't trust him an inch, but he made a handsome escort for a party and, if you didn't take him seriously, he could be fun in small doses.

Lang wasn't in evidence when she and Cary arrived. Cary's father bowed over her hand, exclaiming softly, and she rather enjoyed the kiss on her fingers he was giving her. It made her want to laugh, but she liked it, too.

'Enjoy yourselves,' he said to her and Cary, looking satisfied.

They danced and talked and drank, and Lang hadn't put in an appearance after two hours, so she guessed he wasn't coming and tried to speculate on his reason for passing up the party. Cary was curious, too. He kept making little jokes about it.

When Lang did walk in, he was alone and in evening dress, and made a polite excuse about having had an earlier appointment. His grey eyes skated coldly over Nicola; and Cary noticed that, as fast as a fox after a rabbit where Lang was concerned, and asked lightly: 'Are you and Lang on bad terms at the moment?'

She knew he was hoping they were and she just laughed. 'No more than usual.'

Lang's moods were known. Cary was disappointed. He danced with her held close to him, whispering intimately in her ear, and Lang stood with his back to them and wasn't even looking in their direction. He talked to old Lucci and drank whisky as though it had just been invented. Nicola frowned as she shot him yet another look. Lucci was smiling like a tiger that's swallowed a kid and listening hard. When Cary and Nicola came nearer, dancing, she deliberately stopped, saying: 'Can we have a rest, Cary?'

Lang didn't turn his head. He drank some more whisky and Mr Lucci threw his son a look which told him to keep Nicola away, but she ignored Cary's rapid suggestion of going off to have some more of the cold buffet. Joining Lang and Mr Lucci, she gave the older man a wide smile.

'What a super party, Mr Lucci.'

'Super,' said Lang with sneering sarcasm.

She heard the thickened note of his voice with dismay. He really had been drinking, she thought. Lang rarely drank much; he was a sociable drinker who knew when to stop, but she had a strong feeling that tonight he had been drinking before he arrived.

Looking impatiently at him, she said: 'Will you get me a drink, Cary, please?'

He went off with reluctance and his father compressed his full lips as he looked at Nicola. She glanced over his shoulder at the door. 'You're wanted, I think, Mr Lucci.'

He turned, frowning. There was a man glancing in at the crowded room.

'He waved to you just now,' Nicola lied.

Mr Lucci moved away towards the door and she hurriedly said to Lang: 'Take me home.'

'Bored with Cary, are you?' he asked with a crooked little smile.

'You're nearly drunk,' she said frankly. 'And you'd better get out of here before Lucci takes you apart and shakes every last drop of information out of you.'

'I am not drunk,' he said with careful enunciation. 'I am perfectly sober, thank you.'

Cary was coming back and so was his father at a very hurried pace. 'Lang, take me home!' Nicola hissed, grabbing his arm.

He laughed darkly. 'I wouldn't want to spoil Cary's fun.'

She felt like stamping on his foot. For a second she

looked at him furiously. 'Don't be a fool,' she muttered under her breath.

Cary and his father got there at the same time and Mr Lucci had a wary look, as though he knew she had got rid of him deliberately.

Lang put his glass down. 'We're just off,' he said. 'Super party.'

The sarcasm of that was aimed more at her than at the Lucci family. Cary looked at her indignantly. 'Your drink,' he said, trying to thrust the glass into her hand. He gave Lang a tight smile. 'Come on, Lang, I brought Nicky to the party, I'll take her home.'

'No, I will,' said Lang, giving Cary a sardonic little smile. 'That's the plum job and I get it.'

She went out of the room with him, relieved to get him away as safely as she had, and it was only as he drove away that the penny dropped. She stiffened and turned to stare at him. He was driving and whistling through his teeth in a way she recognised.

'You lying swine!' she burst out. 'You're not the least bit drunk!'

He turned his black head, grinning. 'I told you I wasn't.'

'You made me think you were! And you meant to do it.'

He whistled softly without answering.

'Take me back,' she insisted.

'I'm taking you home,' Lang told her smoothly. He gave her an oblique quick smile. 'What a loyal little girl you are—how lucky I can rely on you.'

Nicola seethed, her teeth tight, and heard him start

to laugh. 'Two can launch campaigns,' Lang said softly a moment later, and she pretended not to hear or understand.

When he stopped outside her flat she dived for the door, but his hand shot across her and held the handle. She stiffened. 'Let me out!'

He turned her, struggling, and she saw his eyes gleaming in the darkness. 'You look very sexy tonight, Nicky,' he whispered, not coming any closer but looking at her in a way that made her pulses roar with reaction.

'A tan suits you,' he said softly. 'Your skin's like a peach.' He lowered his head and she felt him breathing just below her ear, his lips brushing her neck. 'Oh, Nicky, the scent of your skin drives me mad,' he muttered unevenly, and his hands moved, pushing her back against the seat.

Panic streaked through her. She had no time to work out how to evade him. She looked up, protesting, and then his mouth fastened on hers and crushed it hungrily, silencing her muffled words.

She had instinctively put up her hands to thrust him away, but as the kiss deepened, her hands began shifting against him in restless, trembling excitement.

Lang shifted, pressing her back with the weight of his body, and her mind clouded with the suffocating fumes of passion. She gave up and gave in—knowing what she was doing and no longer caring because the burning sensation which he had created in her destroyed all her ability to fight.

While Lang kissed her demandingly she slowly began to undo his shirt. She felt him tense from head to foot. Her fingers were shaking as she moved them down his body, they fumbled for what seemed like years before they could free the buttons.

Lang's tongue was delicately teasing the inside of her lip. She shuddered with pleasure and returned the little caress. Against her mouth Lang groaned, 'Nicky, Nicky,' and she weakly whispered, 'Make love to me, Lang.' She had finally undone his shirt and with a trembling hand she pushed it free of his body.

Sliding her hand inside his shirt, she stared through the shadows in the car at the hollowed line of his collarbone. The wiry dark hair which curled up the centre of his chest tingled against her exploring fingers. Lang lifted his head to stare down at her, but she barely realised it.

She was touching him, at last. She couldn't stop trembling because the physical obsession which had held her for months was in total control of her now. She ran her fingers caressingly along the smooth strong shoulder, touched his throat, moved her hands up and down his deeply breathing chest and felt the heavy thud of his heart knocking under her palms.

Her skin was flushed with fever. Her lips were parted on a stifled moan. Closing her eyes, she fell against him and began to kiss his neck, his shoulder; her mouth open, lips shaking.

Lang didn't move. He just leaned there, not responding. Suddenly he flung her back and she looked at him dazedly, her eyes snapping open. Her skin was burning, her body melting. She met his stare in complete bewilderment.

'You little bitch,' he muttered, his eyes like knives.

She looked blankly at him. What was wrong? Why was he looking at her like that?

'I told myself you wouldn't,' Lang grated harshly. 'I told myself you were teasing me, deliberately trying to make me jealous, but you did, didn't you? How could you do it? How could you do this to me?'

'What are you talking about?' Her whisper was husky with the aroused desire she was still feeling.

His lips twisted in an angry sneer. 'You know what I'm talking about. You think I can't feel the difference?'

'Difference?' she asked in bewilderment.

'The way you were—the way you are now,' he said in sudden fierceness. 'You really think I'd need to have it spelt out for me? You meant me to know—you've made it very clear. The first time I touched you, you blushed like a schoolgirl and went into a state of panic. I could hear your heart racing away. I only had to look at you when I wasn't dressed to have you go scarlet. You wouldn't have touched me like that a month ago. You've been having lessons, haven't you?' His harsh, biting voice stopped abruptly and she saw his throat move, as though he swallowed painfully.

Her eyes had opened wide, her face burning with shock and sheer embarrassment.

Lang stared and his mouth twisted tormentedly. 'Yes,' he muttered. 'I thought so. In Spain, was it? That fellow I saw you with at the airport?'

Realising what he believed had happened, Nicola looked away, biting her lip. He caught her shoulders viciously and shook her.

'Lang, you're hurting!' she winced.

'Hurting?' He laughed savagely. 'Hurting? You turn me down and then deliberately go to bed with someone else and complain that I'm hurting you?'

Nicola couldn't think of a thing to say. She had acted on impulse when she let him think she was going to Spain with James. It had been a sudden, wild inspiration and now she wished she had held her tongue. She was too stupefied with shock to be able to think clearly, staring back at his dark face, shaking, and the more she trembled the more Lang's face tightened.

'Coldbloodedly,' he grated out. 'You did it in cold blood, and we both know why, don't we? You were punishing me. You meant to hurt me as much as you could. Well, I hope you're satisfied. I hope it was worth it.' She saw his mouth move convulsively, toughen and level.

She hated the glittering darkness of his eyes, the pierce of anger and contempt in them. 'Lang——' she began huskily, putting up her hand to touch him, and he shoved her hand away as if he could not bear the touch of it.

'You little bitch,' he said through his teeth. 'Keep all that for him. Don't touch me!'

Nicola winced and then began to feel the flow of anger in her own veins. She sat up and Lang shot back into his own seat. 'Who the hell do you think you are?' Nicola demanded furiously. 'Talking to me like that, accusing me, behaving as though you had some right to criticise what I do—If I chose to go to bed with a dozen different men it would be no affair of yours!'

He turned a grim face towards her. 'If you'd wanted him, I'd agree, but you wanted me and you only did it to punish me.'

'How many women have there been in your life since I met you?' she threw back jealously.

'That has nothing to do with it.'

'Oh, no, of course, it wouldn't have. You can do as you like, I suppose.'

'They none of them mattered a row of beans and you know it. I had an arrangement with them—one that suited me and suited them. There was never any suggestion that it meant more. They have nothing to do with this.'

'But you did make love to them,' she said bitterly. 'Why is it all right for you but not for me?'

Lang's eyes flashed. 'Because you love me!' he shouted, and then stopped speaking, staring at her, his colour flooding away. He looked as though he had shocked himself, as though he hadn't known what he was saying until now.

Nicola found it so painful that she felt tears pricking at the back of her eyes. She had never even said that to herself. A physical obsession, she had told herself, that was all it was—and, instead, it had been love, and now he had said it out loud and she couldn't even deny it. She loved him; fiercely, desperately, and Lang knew it.

She drew a shaky breath and forced her trembling

limbs to be still. 'Well, as you said yourself, love doesn't last. I'll get over it,' she said. 'I'll learn not to care twopence for you if it kills me.'

She swung to open the door and got out. Lang was sitting there, his head turned away. Nicola looked with cold numbness at his black head and walked away.

# CHAPTER NINE

SHE couldn't sleep that night. She turned and sighed on the pillow, fighting down the pain which was filling every corner of her. Inch by inch over the past months Lang had been driving her back from the position of calm neutrality towards him which she had assumed long ago. He had forced her to admit she was attracted to him, and now he had forced her to admit she loved him.

He had looked as shaken as she was when he said it. His eyes had been almost dazed with shock as he stared at her.

Perhaps he hadn't even known himself until that moment. Had the realisation been at the back of his mind without his being aware of it? Had it come out under the stress of his anger, taking him as much by surprise as her?

He had said he didn't believe in love and she knew he had been speaking the truth. But he had nevertheless known she loved him. During the years she worked for him they had come very close; you couldn't work that intimately with a man without getting inside his head. She had learnt to handle him, to watch him with laughter behind her eyes, and it was always dangerous for a woman to believe she can manage a man. It makes her feel possessive towards him.

Lang's outrage and bitter anger over what he imagined she had done in Spain made her pulses quicken. Lang had been jealous—he had made no secret of it. He might have had no intention of marrying her, but he wanted her and he was furious because he believed someone else had talked her into bed.

She should never have been so weak as to give in to the driving, hungry need to touch him. Even when he made love to her in the bedroom at Sillory, she had somehow managed to control her own desire, and Lang had recognised that she was inexperienced, untouched. Tonight her reactions had been very different and she knew it, despising herself for the way she had behaved.

She had been keeping him firmly at bay for weeks. Why hadn't she gone on doing so?

What a fool I am, she thought, staring into the darkness. What a weak-minded fool! She winced with shame as she remembered herself moaning out a plea for Lang to make love to her. At the time she had been shaking with excitement, all her common sense lost in a melting need to experience the satisfaction she knew his body would give her.

Even now the thought of it could make her senses leap and quiver in aroused desire.

She covered her face with her hands, groaning.

Lang knew she loved him. That really hurt. For him to know, to be aware of her feelings, was the most humiliating thing that had ever happened to her.

No wonder he had been so confident of persuading

her to sleep with him. If he had known, subconsciously or otherwise, that she was not merely physically attracted to him but seriously in love with him, he must have thought it would be a walk-over.

Lang had been concentrating all his attention on her for weeks. He had broken with Lois in the spring and now it was August, and there hadn't been anyone else in his life, so far as she knew. If Lang had picked up another of his damned blondes she would have heard about it from Andrew or Monica. Lang had been blonde-less for months and he had been conducting a careful campaign against her since June, focusing all his sexual weapons on her. Frustrated, losing patience, growing more urgent as the weeks went by, he would have had the ground cut from under his feet when he thought she had been seduced by James.

'You meant to hurt me,' he had accused, and she would love to believe she had because that would mean she meant more to Lang than another conquest, but she strongly suspected that he had meant that she had hurt his sexual pride.

Good, she thought bitterly. I hope I have. I hope I've smashed his ego into a thousand pieces. Her own ego had taken a real beating. Knowing that Lang was aware of the way she felt about him left her feeling sick and humiliated. She would far rather have him glare at her with that black rage than have him smile with the gleaming amusement she had seen in his grey eyes once he realised she was wide open to him.

She was pale under her smooth tan when she went into the office next morning, and horribly nervous of the reception she was likely to get from Lang.

He wasn't there, to her relief. She started work, wanting for the sound of his movements, her stomach clenched in sickening anxiety as she kept glancing at the clock.

When he did arrive her neck beat with a fierce, painful pulse. Lang glanced across at her, his face coolly unreadable, and gave her a nod. She waited for him to say something, but when he did speak it was about work and there wasn't a flicker of personal feeling in his hard face.

As the day wore on, Nicola began to realise that he was going to pretend it hadn't happened. He didn't mean to re-open the subject. He was treating her with polite iciness and she was driven back into anger herself.

The trembling anxiety went. A chill bitterness took its place. If that's the way he wants it, she thought, her head bent over her desk, that's the way he's going to have it.

Andrew came in and spoke to him and Lang talked in a curt, level voice, getting a surprised, puzzled look from Andrew before he went out.

It was the longest day of Nicola's life. She had never imagined that she would hate to hear Lang close doors quietly, speak in a clear, calm voice, but she discovered that she found the change intolerable.

She went home to an empty flat and a sensation of dull weariness. She listened to music on her stereo and read a book of which she took in very little. When she went to bed she was tired after her previous sleepless night and fell asleep quite soon but she had tense, alarming dreams which kept waking her in a trembling state of nerves.

Next day Lang was already at his desk when she arrived. He was as coolly remote as he had been the day before and gradually she knew that the distance between them was going to be permanent.

Lang wasn't saying anything because there was nothing he was going to say. He had cut her out. His grey eyes were blank when they looked at her, his voice level and polite. They might have been strangers.

It cut her to the quick. She was miserable under her calm face. It cost her a good deal to carry on working, knowing that he was so far away.

The rapid, impatient drive of his manner had become a contained curtness which was worse than a slap across the face because of all that it implied.

Day followed day and nothing changed. Andrew commented on it curiously. 'Lang's very quiet these days. I hope he isn't sickening for something.'

Nicola didn't answer that. What could she say? 'He's working very hard,' she did say later, when Andrew pressed her.

'Still busy with Fairfax?' Andrew asked.

She nodded. In fact she had seen James that week—he had rung up several times and at last she had accepted a date to go to dinner with him. They had spent the evening talking about architecture. Nicola encouraged James to talk about his profession because when he was explaining the finer points of space-in-relation-to-people, he wasn't trying to kiss her.

'If you ever feel like sailing,' Andrew mumbled vaguely, and she gave him a little smile.

'Not the weather, really, is it?'

The summer had drifted into autumn. Leaves hung like tattered yellow banners along the branches of trees in the London parks. The busy, running river had a deeper swell to it, and the wind blew in chill gusts from the water. She walked to work some mornings in swirling white mist which lifted slowly as the sun warmed the city.

'I suppose not,' Andrew admitted reluctantly. He hadn't much imagination and all he knew was that Nicola liked sailing. It had been their main bond.

Lang walked in and stopped, seeing his brother hanging round her desk.

'Do you want me, Andy?' he asked curtly, and Andrew burbled nothing in particular before he bolted.

Lang turned cold eyes on her. 'Any messages?'

'No,' she said, equally icy.

He nodded and went back to his own office. Nicola made lurid faces at his door, feeling like throwing things at it. The slow drift of the year towards the winter echoed the feeling inside her.

She was drifting, too. She accepted more dates with James because anything was better than sitting at home in her quiet flat hearing the clock tick ruthlessly through her life. James expected to be able to kiss her, of course, and she had to let him. It didn't mean a thing and she couldn't make herself pretend it did. She was relieved that he didn't press her any harder because she knew she couldn't possibly go to bed with him. That was too much for her to bear. She liked him, but she knew it would make her ill to let him do more than kiss her.

In late October she and James were at the first night of a new play when they saw Lang in the bar during the interval. He wasn't alone. Monica and the beautiful Toby were with him and Lang had the look of suppressed fury which he always wore when his sister was nagging him about something.

'Hey,' said James, staring. 'Isn't that your boss?'

'Yes.' Nicola hoped James wouldn't draw Lang's attention to them. She knew he hadn't seen them yet and she hoped he wouldn't do so.

Monica was talking, her hand on Lang's arm, while Toby lounged beside them, gazing around him with a bored expression on his pretty face. Why Monica thought so much of him was incomprehensible, Nicola thought. He was just something malleable for her to push around, presumably. Monica liked running people's lives and most people resisted her attempts to do so, but Toby didn't have the nerve to do more than look helpless and pout. If he had been older, Nicola might have suspected Monica of being in love with him, but whenever she saw them together Monica was bossing him around, more like a mother than a lover.

In his restless sweep of the crowded bar, his eyes came in contact with Nicola. She looked away, but Toby had recognised her. She did not hear what he said to his companions, but she did hear Monica's piercing reply. 'Nicola? Where?'

Lang turned on a reflex movement. His grey eyes

shot across the crowded space and she met them with a peculiar, drowning sensation of sheer craving.

She felt her face flare with colour and looked at Monica instead. Monica beckoned in a peremptory fashion and at last Nicola and James went over to join them.

'Imagine seeing you here,' said Monica, glancing at James.

Nicola introduced him, fighting to stop herself looking at Lang again. He wasn't looking at her; he was twisting his glass in his hand and watching it. James shook hands with Monica and Toby. Lang raised his glass and drained it, then as James turned to offer his hand to him, Lang swung on his heel and walked away.

James looked surprised and then annoyed. Monica stared at Lang's departing back and then turned with narrowed eyes to look at Nicola. Her intuition had picked up signals from Nicola during that weekend at Sillory and now Monica's brain was clicking away like a computer, putting two and two together and making God knew what.

'What's up with him?' Toby asked in his light, drawling voice, and Monica gave Nicola a sharp little smile.

'What indeed?' she shrugged.

Nicola's face was burning. She could not stop the colour mounting in her face and was furious with herself.

The first bell went and she said huskily: 'We must get back, James.'

'What do you think of the play?' Monica demanded,

detaining her with a hand on her arm.

'Very good,' Nicola muttered.

'Are you enjoying it, Mr Fairfax?' Monica asked James, and he said it was better than he had expected.

'Nicky twisted my arm to come, but I'm glad I did,' he said, and gave her a grin because it was true, he hadn't been that keen.

The second bell went and everybody was moving out of the bar. James put a hand round Nicola's waist. 'Time to move, angel.'

She smiled at Monica. 'Nice to see you again, Mrs Finister.'

Lang had walked up behind them. She didn't turn her head, but she knew he was there and her breathing had become painful. James guided her out of the bar and she hoped he could not hear the fierce pounding of her heart.

She barely knew what happened in the second act of the play; the words washed over her head. She aped James's reactions automatically, smiling if he smiled, listening with apparent fascination when he did. All the time she was remembering over and over again Lang's harsh frown and the abrupt movement of his body as James turned towards him. Lang had refused to shake hands with James and she speculated feverishly on what that revealed of his feelings.

They didn't run into Lang and Monica again. After the play, James took her home and kissed her goodnight, then Nicola went into her flat to spend the night tossing restlessly as she tried to decipher the meaning of that expression on Lang's face.

She went to the office next morning in a state of suspension, not sure what she was going to find when she saw him. She knew the moment he walked into her office and she met the flash of his eyes. The ice had cracked at last, but now Lang's anger was out in the open. He was grim, moving with the old impatient, forceful stride, his body like taut wire.

He began sniping at her from the first second. 'You're late. I expect to find my letters open and sorted when I come in, not to have to do it myself.'

Nicola glanced at her watch to cover her alarm. It was exactly nine. 'I'm not late,' she started, and he cut in on her furiously.

'You are. Get here on time in future. Find me the three memos which came last week from Gloucester— I want to sort that out before I start on dictation.'

She had never thought she would ache to hear him roaring at her, but although he was using a terse, objectionable voice she was so relieved to see this thaw that she almost smiled. Lang cloaked in ice was far more worrying than Lang snarling like an unfed tiger.

She found the memos and handed them to him. His eyes shot to her face. 'What are you grinning at?' he barked. 'Tell me the joke. But it had better be funny.'

'I'm not grinning,' she protested.

'Oh, yes, you are.' He dropped the memos and stood up, dwarfing her, his eyes violent. 'Do you think I don't know you're laughing at me?'

'Would you rather I hit you?' she asked angrily, her own temper shooting up.

Lang's teeth came together. He glared at her for a

few seconds, then said in barbed softness : 'Try it. Just
try it, Nicky.'

Her hands clenched at her sides. He held her eyes and
she looked back at him, wishing she had the nerve to
slap him and afraid to dare. There was a glint in his
eye suddenly that warned her that if she did, Lang
would come back with action she might find disturbing.

Dropping her glance at last, she said shakily : 'Shall
I get the Gloucester firm on the line?'

'Yes,' Lang said on a strange note.

Nicola retreated nervously while he watched her.
Andrew dropped in, but as soon as he heard Andrew's
voice Lang bellowed for him and with a startled glance
at her Andrew went through to Lang's office. She heard
Lang snapping at him for a while, then Andrew came
back and gave her a wide grin, whispering, 'I see he's
himself again.' Like her, Andrew was oddly relieved,
as though Lang had been ill and was now over the
worst.

The day whirled past. Lang had a blitz on a wide
range of matters he had been neglecting lately. He kept
Nicola running to and from the office files all the time
and she had a sandwich at lunchtime rather than go out
for lunch because her desk was flooded with a tidal
wave of paper.

Lang went out and was gone for several hours.
When he came back he was wearing a red carnation in
his buttonhole and she looked at it sharply. It wasn't
a red rose, but she felt her stomach sink as though
she was in a lift which had dropped abruptly.

She glanced up and Lang was watching her with a shuttered, thoughtful face.

Who had he had lunch with? she wondered jealously.

That evening as she got up to go he came into her office and asked tartly: 'What are *you* doing?'

'I was here at nine,' Nicola snapped. 'It's six o'clock now.'

'Clock-watching?' he demanded. 'Got a date with Fairfax again, have you?'

'No, I'm going to have a long bath and an early night,' Nicola bit out furiously.

'Is he tiring you out?' Lang said in barbed mockery, and she didn't answer, walking away with her head held high.

After a light supper she had the leisurely bath she had promised herself, soaking in fragrant water, and was on the point of washing her hair when the doorbell went.

James! she thought irritably. He had asked if he could come round and she had refused. She tied her dressing-gown around her waist and went to the door, pulling it open with sharp words on her lips.

It wasn't James standing on the doorstep. It was Lang, and she was so taken aback that she stared at him in disbelief. He was wearing his dark suit, but he had removed the tie he had been wearing earlier and his shirt was open at the neck. For a moment Nicola wondered if he had been drinking, then as he stepped forward she tried to close the door. Lang shouldered it open and shot past her. Closing the door as she began to protest angrily, he leaned on it and eyed her derisively. 'Surprised to see me?'

'What are you doing here?'

'I've come to my senses,' he said, and she looked at him with total bewilderment.

'I've been a fool,' he told her.

Her heart suddenly missed a beat.

'It doesn't matter a damn,' said Lang, his voice deepening. 'Only one thing matters.'

Nicola was wary. She took a step backwards, not taking her eyes off him. She had a strong feeling he was about to pounce.

'What are you talking about?' she asked.

'You know what I'm talking about,' Lang said drily. 'There isn't much about me you don't know, is there? I always swore I'd never let a woman get me under her thumb and I still damned well don't know how you did it, but you did.'

The fierce sweet pain which shot through her almost made her cry out, but she managed to look blankly at him. 'What?'

'Don't pretend to be dumb, Nicky,' he said with a sardonic gleam. 'The more I know you, the more I realise just how damned clever you are. For months you've been dangling me on a piece of string. Isn't it time you hauled me in?'

'Go away,' she said desperately.

She had backed and Lang had advanced and now she was against the wall, all her paths of escape cut off. Lang put a hand on either side of her head and leaned there, looking at her, his face inches away. Her eyes darkened, his nearness oppressive. She looked at the hard, strong mouth and trembled.

'That's more like it,' he whispered.

The door bell rang and she jumped. Lang straightened, his lips curling back from his teeth in a snarl. 'Who the hell's that?'

Their eyes met and Nicola looked away.

'Fairfax,' he muttered. 'Well, I'll soon get rid of him.'

She leaned on the wall, watching him move tautly to the door. She should stop him. She should tell him to go. But she didn't move, watching the angry set of his shoulders weakly.

He pulled open the door and she heard James say in a surprised voice, 'Oh, hello. Nicky there?'

'No,' Lang said coldly.

'Oh.' James hesitated, clearly not believing him. She heard him move as though he were trying to walk past Lang. 'Well, I'll wait,' he said.

'You won't,' Lang informed him through his teeth.

Nicola could see the black back of his head. She could see the poised tension in his body. She could hear the vicious undertone of hostility.

So could James.

'Now look here——' he began, but Lang cut him short.

'Clear off. Consider yourself lucky I don't knock you down the stairs!'

He slammed the door and before he had moved the bell rang again, loudly, furiously.

'Don't,' Nicky begged as she saw the way Lang pulled the door open again.

He ignored her. James came through the door at a rush, saying angrily: 'Who the hell d'you think you are?'

'I gave you fair warning,' Lang said with dangerous satisfaction. Nicola started forward in alarm, but she was too late. Lang's fist shot out and James fell backwards through the door. She heard the thud of his head hitting something and the muffled curses which followed.

'Stay away from her or next time I'll beat you to a pulp!' Lang told him savagely before he slammed the door again.

Nicola ran to open it again and Lang stopped her with a hand which bit into her arm.

'Where do you think you're going?'

'James may be hurt,' she burst out anxiously.

'I damned well hope so,' gritted Lang. 'I hit him hard enough.'

'You can't do things like that!' Nicola protested.

She heard James moving outside. 'You'll be sorry if I set eyes on you again, you swine,' he said loudly, but then he slowly made his way down stairs, stumbling.

Lang turned a sardonic face on her. 'Your gallant lover,' he bit out. 'Gives up easily, doesn't he?'

Her face burned. 'You can go too,' she shouted. 'Go on, get out of here!'

'Oh, no, Nicky,' he said softly. 'I've dealt with him and now I'm going to deal with you.'

'Oh, you beat women up too, do you?' She faced him defiantly.

'Not normally,' he agreed. 'But for you I'm going to make an exception.'

She didn't really think he meant it, but she didn't care for something in the glitter of the grey eyes.

Warily she began to edge away. Lang watched her very casually, his face hard.

Nicola panicked. She fled, and it was not until too late that it dawned on her that she had made a mistake.

Lang was right behind her and he laughed under his breath. As she stopped dead, trembling, he mocked: 'Keep going, darling. You're going in the right direction.'

'Stop it!' she flared, facing him. 'You're not frightening me.'

His smile had gone. His face was grim, now, and she had lied—he was frightening her. She was scared stiff as she met the bitter hardness of his stare.

'Get it over with, Nicky,' he warned in a crisp voice. 'Take your punishment and let's get it out of the way.'

She was shaking now, staring at him with enormous blue eyes, her hands clutching at her dressing-gown. 'Lang, don't,' she whispered as she looked at him.

'You deserve it,' Lang bit out. 'You've been a stupid little bitch and I'm going to give you the slapping of your life!'

That was not what she had imagined was on his mind and she stared in stupified disbelief. Lang took a stride and the next moment she was being carried, kicking and struggling, into her bedroom.

# CHAPTER TEN

'DON'T you dare!' she shrieked as he sat down on the edge of her bed and held her face down over his knee. His hand held her by the nape and however hard she struggled she couldn't get up.

'Oh!' she squealed as the first slap stung. Lang's arm rose and fell and Nicola writhed and gave angry, humiliated cries of pain. He wasn't just playing; he was slapping her hard, intending to hurt.

He was breathing heavily as he stopped. He turned her over, then his arm slid under her and he lifted her towards him. Before she could burst out with bitter complaint, he was kissing her ruthlessly, his lips fierce and hot. For a few seconds Nicola resisted him with every ounce of her strength, then she gave up the useless contest and her arms curved round his bent head.

Lang murmured huskily against her bruised lips. 'Nicky, Nicky.' His hand opened her dressing-gown and smoothly slid inside it. She arched in piercing, compelling excitement as she felt his fingers fondling the warm swell of her breast. Her dressing-gown fell wide open and Lang looked down at her yielding body. Nicola opened her eyes reluctantly to watch him. His eyes slowly wandered down the pale curve from breast to thigh and she heard him draw a sharp breath.

'I seem to have been waiting for you for years, Nicky,' he whispered.

'Not as long as I've waited for you,' she said, abandoning all pretence.

His eyes flicked back to her face. His smile was wry. 'Has it been a long time, Nicky?'

'My whole life,' she said on a wrenched sigh.

Lang gently lifted her off his knees and laid her on the bed. She didn't move, watching him as he began to take off his clothes. For so long she had fought the desire to watch him, but now she openly stared as he undid his shirt and slid out of it. Lang glanced at her, eyes glinting, beginning to smile.

His hands were shaking slightly, but there was a teasing understanding in his look. 'Enjoying yourself, darling?'

'Yes,' she said frankly, half smiling, half serious. Her blood was singing in her ears in a way she recognised. Her skin was overheated and her mouth dry. She looked at the long, lean body with passionate intensity as though memorising the way the dark hair curled down the middle of his deep chest, the flat planes of his stomach, the strong loins and thighs.

Her gaze crept back up to his face and Lang was watching her in his turn. He was breathing thickly. His eyes burnt as he moved towards her.

As his body covered hers she gave a wild hoarse moan of pleasure and he crushed her mouth under his lips, his hands sliding strokingly from her trembling shoulder to her thigh. She was shaking so much she felt dizzy. She had her arms round him, her hands pressing down the powerful line of his back, following the spine and teasing the short fine hairs which marked it. She felt him shift his mouth to her throat and the soft heated movement of his lips sent stabbing pleasure through her.

'How did I ever come to think you were too thin?' he said, lifting his head to look into her eyes.

She lazily moved one hand up his back and saw the excited flicker of his eyes. Raising her head from the pillow, she brushed his warm shoulder with her lips and the feel of his skin under her mouth sent her crazy. She began kissing his neck, moving restlessly, and Lang forced her back on the pillow and kissed her mouth hard.

'Yes, darling,' he muttered, as though she had said something.

His fingers smoothed down her thighs. She was trembling helplessly as she let him part them and it was only as Lang slid between them that her body tensed in a violent stiffening jerk.

'Relax, darling,' he said, giving her a surprised look.

She bit down on her lip. He was hurting her badly and she struggled to relax her tense muscles.

'What's wrong?' Lang asked, frowning. 'Nicky——' and then she heard him draw a long hard breath.

'Nicky!' he said again on a sharp, hoarse note.

She couldn't meet his eyes. She was very flushed and still trembling from head to foot. Lang said something violent.

His hand shot out to push up her chin. 'Look at me,' he said harshly and she nervously met his narrowed eyes.

'Are you still a virgin?' The question shot out of him on a rising fierceness.

She slid her eyes sideways, not able to speak.

'You lied, didn't you? You lied to me. You let me think you'd been to bed with him to punish me.' His hands bit into her shoulders and shook her furiously. 'Didn't you?'

Nicola was too scared to answer. Lang looked like a man on the point of murder and she was petrified. She put a hand over her eyes to shut out the sight of that taut, angry face.

'You little bitch,' Lang said hoarsely. 'You've put me through months of hell and all the time you were lying to me.' He lifted her as though she were a rag doll and shook her again, and she looked at him through her fingers like a child, wincing.

Lang dropped her and then pulled her hand away to uncover her face.

Nicola whispered shakily, 'I love you.'

Lang stared at her with fixed, glittering eyes. His face unlocked from the anger which had held it. 'You silly little fool,' he muttered unevenly. 'I've a good mind to give you another slapping. Don't you realise what it did to me to believe that another man had been the first?'

'You jumped to conclusions, I didn't tell you I'd done it,' she protested. 'I just didn't tell you I hadn't.'

'The idea that you'd cold-bloodedly gone to bed with someone else when I knew ...' He broke off and looked at her, his mouth twisting. 'When I knew you loved me,' he said huskily.

She flinched.

'Don't look like that,' Lang muttered. 'Don't, my darling.'

The pulse in her neck beat with a fierce agony. She stared at him, her lips trembling.

Lang made a strange, wry little gesture, his shoulders lifting. 'I find it hard to say,' he said, his face filling with dark blood, his eyes shifting as though he couldn't look at her.

Nicola's breathing seemed to stop. Lang flicked a glance at her and then his eyes stayed on her face, intent. 'All right,' he said. 'It's mutual.'

She was torn between tears and laughter. The half-sulky look of his mouth made her want to giggle.

'There's no need to tell me fairy stories, Lang,' she said with wry amusement.

'Do you think I want to admit it?' He grimaced. 'I feel a bloody fool. I'd have put money on it that this would never happen to me.'

She smiled at him and Lang lowered his head and took her mouth fiercely. The kiss made her shudder with passion and when he drew his mouth away it was to bury his face in her throat.

He began muttering into her skin in a low, hoarse voice, and she strained to hear and understand what he was telling her.

'I love you, Nicky. I didn't even know it until I thought Fairfax had got to you. I couldn't stand the thought of someone else holding you in his arms. It had to be me. I think I've felt like that for a long time. I know I was knocked for six when I saw Andy kissing

you in your office the day you handed me your notice.
It had been very quiet in there for a while and I sat
there, trying to pretend I wasn't listening, fighting not
to get up to go and see what the hell was going on.
When I did open the door and saw ...' He broke off
and groaned. 'I felt very odd. I went back in my office
and sat there and I felt sick. And I didn't know why.'

Nicola trembled, her arms round his back.

'After I'd held you myself, down at Monica's, I
knew it had to be me. Your response was so passionate
—I knew I could have you and I was going crazy just
thinking about it. It was obvious I'd be the first, and
I liked that. I'd never thought about it before with anyone but I loved it.' He drew a long harsh breath. 'And
then when you got back from Spain I saw you with him
at the airport and suspicion started eating away at me.
I told myself you were teasing me. I wouldn't believe
you could do it, and then in the car that night the way
you were touching me was so different. God, I went
wild! The very idea that you had let him have you
when I knew you were mine made me want to throw
up.'

He lifted his head, his eyes closed, his face grim. 'I
thought of nothing else day after day. I told myself I'd
been wrong, you didn't love me, and that made me
even more sick. Then you looked at me last night and
it was in your eyes.'

It was in her eyes now and she wasn't trying to hide
it any more. Lang watched the passion burning inside
her and his body began to tremble. 'You don't know
what you do to me,' he said huskily.

'Don't I?' She put her hand up and let it sweep down over him, feeling the fierce clench of his flesh as she touched it. He gasped and groaned.

'Nicky—my God, Nicky!'

Her blue eyes teased, incited. 'And I haven't had any lessons from anyone but you,' she mocked, her voice drowsy with passionate heat.

'The mind reels,' said Lang, but his body was stirring and hardened as she stroked it and she heard the breathless excitement in his voice with a sense of power.

'I didn't need lessons—I just did what I'd been dying to do for months,' she admitted, smiling at him. Even if his love wasn't going to last, any pain he inflicted, physical or emotional, was outweighed by the sheer necessity of having him possess her.

'Shameless,' Lang whispered, laughing, then as her caress became more urgent said huskily, 'I won't hurt you, darling,' his hands moving intimately on her.

'Yes, hurt me,' she moaned feverishly, because even now she was looking forward to the day when he would tire of her, and she was already dying of pain. She wound her arms around him and accepted all the pain with a faint moan. Lang stiffened and looked at her face in taut, searching comprehension.

'Don't, Nicky,' he said huskily.

She laughed with a bitter amusement. 'In three months' time I'll be sending red roses to myself. Start as you mean to go on, damn you.'

'O.K., I'm a high risk, Nicky,' he said harshly. 'I told you that myself. But I've never been in love before. When I fancied a woman I took her to bed, but I never for a second thought I was in love with any of them, and I lost interest very rapidly.'

'I know,' she said. 'I've got three months. So don't waste any of it talking.'

Lang gave a wry grin at that. 'When they tell you about love they talk a lot about moonlight and roses, but they never tell you that what love does to you is eat at your guts when you suspect another man has had your woman, make you stay awake half the night sweating with pain and rage.' He swallowed, shuddering. 'Never do that to me again, Nicky.'

She watched him, torn between hope and despair.

'Take a risk on me, Nicky. I'll admit, it's a gamble— I've no way of knowing if the way I feel now is going to last for ever. It's all as new to me as it is to you. This is my first love affair too. I've taken quite a battering from you since I first started looking at you and thinking that I'd like to have you. We know each other so well in every other way. You knew exactly where to place your daggers, didn't you? I can't hide a thing from you.'

'You've managed it lately,' she said in dry emphasis.

He shook his head, his mouth crooked. 'I don't believe it. You knew what you'd done to me.' He glanced wryly into her eyes. 'You did it deliberately, don't tell me you didn't. You knew I was so jealous I could scarcely bear to look at you. You were punishing me.'

'You were very quiet,' she commented.

'I was struggling,' he muttered. 'Not waving but drowning, Nicky. I didn't want to face some hard facts. They were bad nights I had recently. I knew damned well I'd heard the cage door clang, but I didn't want to admit I couldn't get out.'

She laughed, her body relaxing from the pain which had been holding it. 'Are you telling me you think this time it may last? What if you get bored with me?'

'I thought of that,' he grimaced. 'I told myself I would, but I couldn't make myself believe it because in two years you've never bored me. You've amused me, you've annoyed me, but you've never bored me. I kept remembering when I was ill . . .'

'When you had that little cold?' she asked, and he gave her a veiled look from below his lashes.

'No provocation, Nicky. When I was ill I wanted you around, and normally I can't stand women cluttering up the place unless I'm in the mood. I certainly wasn't in the mood just then—but it irritated me because you wouldn't stay. I know you say I wasn't ill, but I felt terrible.'

She watched his dark face, remembering the sulky irritation with which he had tried to get her to fuss over him. He had behaved with a childish demand for her attention that had surprised her then, and looking back she wondered that it hadn't struck her before. Lang was always so careful to keep his women out of his flat. He didn't want them getting ideas about domesticating him. He didn't want them cooking for him or sneaking themselves into his life. She had merely thought that his unusual behaviour was due to his cold.

'Most girls can't wait to get into the kitchen and

show what fantastic cooks they are—I practically had to go on my knees to get you to make me scrambled eggs.'

He looked down at her amused face. 'You were always laughing at me. Do you think I didn't know? All your little campaigns to get me into line! You were running my life and you'd got me so tame I was even damned well enjoying it.' He kissed her cheek, her ear, her neck, murmuring fiercely to her.

'I never knew how badly I needed you until you walked out on me. I knew you were angry with me because I'd kissed Caroline and that had made me wonder, but when you said you were going I was shaken. I couldn't believe you meant it. I waited for you to come back, but you didn't. I saw you now and then and you looked right through me. I went crazy thinking of ways to get you back. I hated seeing another girl at your desk. I picked every hole in their work I could. One or two of them were quite efficient, but they weren't you and I couldn't stand the sight of them.'

'You behaved very badly,' Nicola told him, frowning. 'When I saw you with Caroline I wanted to kill you.'

His face was grim. 'I know. You were white. I hated myself—I'd felt no qualms about taking up her very obvious offer until then, but when you looked at me as if you hated me I felt two inches high.'

'Good,' she said, and he looked at her with amusement.

'My God, they say men are tough! Women are deadly. I didn't have a chance, did I? I really got whipped for giving in to temptation. I'd never even thought about what was happening to me until you walked out and I was left facing a damned great hole. My life just fell apart. I told myself I needed you in the office, but I should have known then that I was done for. You made me crawl on my knees before you would come back.'

'It was an expensive lunch,' she admitted. 'But I wouldn't have described it as crawling on your knees. A gesture of contrition, that's what I'd call it.'

Lang kissed her and then kissed her again urgently. 'Nicky. Nicky, let me come home to you every night and bury myself in your body. I've wanted to do that for weeks. Night after night I've walked up and down my flat grinding my teeth and imagining you with Fairfax, and I can't take any more nights without you.'

'Are you asking me to live with you?' she asked softly.

'Marry me,' Lang said. 'You know that's what I mean.'

She smiled at him and his grey eyes flared. 'It's that smile of yours—I should have known better than to let a clever woman take me over, but I was so fascinated by your smile that I didn't see the cage until I was inside.'

'Poor Lang,' she mocked, her heart beating fiercely.

'I believe it was all one of your clever campaigns,' Lang told her. 'You meant to get me and you're like the Mounties—you always get your man.'

She didn't answer, smiling, her fingers stroking down his lean body.

'Mona Lisa,' Lang muttered. 'What are you thinking? Pleased with yourself for pulling it off, are you? I know that honey-sweet look. My God! I ought to. I've seen it over and over again in the past two years and it always means that you've somehow got me to do something I didn't want to do. You're worse than Monica because you're far more dangerous. Monica makes my head ache. You seduce me, with your blue eyes and your soft voice and that deceptive smile of yours.'

Nicola was watching the way his hand moved as he talked, feeling the fierce tingle of pleasure he was giving her.

'I should have locked the door and got under the bed the day I first set eyes on you,' Lang went on. 'Even if I felt like straying I've got a horrible suspicion I wouldn't get an inch from your side.' He put a hand to his throat, frowning. 'I hope to God nobody can see it.'

'What?' she asked, puzzled.

'The collar and leash,' said Lang with a wry emphasis. He looked at her, grinning. 'Admit it, Nicky. I was set up, wasn't I? You've played it superbly and I don't believe it wasn't all a cool plot.'

'There's still time to escape,' Nicola murmured, smiling with her eyes lowered. 'There's the door, Lang. I won't try to stop you going through it.'

'That's the real cunning of it, isn't it? I wouldn't go even if you begged me to. You couldn't get me out of here with a loaded gun aimed at my head. The cage is too invitingly baited.'

She stopped smiling, her face intent. 'I warn you, Lang. If I marry you, I'll never let you go.'

'I know that,' Lang said quietly, looking down into her eyes. 'Why do you think I struggled so hard? I knew the sort of rules you played by and I knew you wouldn't bend or break them for me.'

'You tried to make me,' she commented drily.

'Of course I did,' he grinned. 'What do you think I am? Stupid? But all the time I knew the only thing you'd accept was a permanent relationship.'

She shook her head. 'No, Lang, not that—but love. It was love I wanted and not just three months of bed and board.'

He laughed huskily. 'I do love you, Nicky. More than that—I need you. I saw it suddenly the other day —the only way I was going to be sure of keeping you was to marry you.'

'I knew you only wanted a free housekeeper!'

He laughed but added soberly: 'It's the only guarantee of fidelity I can give you, darling, the fact that I'm too scared of losing you to look at anyone else.'

'No more blondes?'

He laughed. 'They were a taste I'd already begun to lose before I started chasing you. I found I got very bored with them. However pretty they were it got tedious having nothing to do but make love.'

'How sad,' she mocked, her eyes very sharp, and he observed her expression with amusement.

'I've become addicted to women with tongues like razors,' he told her, grinning. 'A dangerous hobby, but I'm hooked on it now.'

'Just don't send me any red roses,' Nicola warned. 'I won't be responsible if you do.'

His eyes smiled at her. 'On our silver wedding anniversary, darling, I'll send you a bushel of them.'

Nicola smiled, content with that, and looked at the smooth width of his shoulders. 'Lang, just one question?'

'Mmm?' he asked, stroking her breast softly.

'Are we going to talk all night?'

His grin widened. 'Not on your life,' he promised, and began to give her lessons in how to make a man happy even in a cage.

## The Mills & Boon Rose is the Rose of Romance

### Look for the Mills & Boon Rose next month

**WHERE THE WOLF LEADS** *by Jane Arbor*
Everybody seemed to behave like sheep where Dracon
Leloupblanc was concerned. And why, thought Tara Dryden
indignantly, should she add herself to their number?

**THE DARK OASIS** *by Margaret Pargeter*
When Mrs Martin's son ran off with Kurt d'Estier's fiancée, she
persuaded her secretary Maxine to go off to Morocco to try to
pacify Kurt.

**BAREFOOT BRIDE** *by Dorothy Cork*
To save face when she found her fiancé strangely unwelcoming,
Amy pretended that she was going to marry the cynical Mike
Saunders instead — then Mike stunned her by taking her up on
it . . .

**A TOUCH OF THE DEVIL** *by Anne Weale*
There was mutual attraction between Joe Crawford and Bianca
— but marriage, Joe made it clear, was not in his mind.

**THE SILVER THAW** *by Betty Neels*
A holiday in Norway was supposed to give Amelia and her fiancé
Tom a chance to get their affairs settled once and for all. But
somehow she found herself seeing far more of Gideon van der
Tolck.

**DANGEROUS TIDE** *by Elizabeth Graham*
Her ex-husband was the last person Toni had expected to meet
on board a cruise ship to Mexico. But he, it appeared, had
expected to meet her . . .

**MARRIAGE IN HASTE** *by Sue Peters*
Trapped in a Far Eastern country on the brink of civil war,
Netta could only manage to escape if she married the mysterious
Joss de Courcy . . .

**THE TENDER LEAVES** *by Essie Summers*
Searching for her father in New Zealand, Maria could have done
without the help of the disapproving Struan Mandeville. But
could she *really* do without Struan?

**LOVE AND NO MARRIAGE** *by Roberta Leigh*
Career woman Samantha swiftly fell in love with Bart Jackson,
who had no time for career girls and thought she was a quiet
little homebody . . .

**THE ICE MAIDEN** *by Sally Wentworth*
Just for an experiment, Gemma and her friends had computerised
the highly eligible Paul Verignac, and Gemma was proceeding to
turn herself into 'his kind of woman' . . .

# Doctor Nurse Romances

and August's
stories of romantic relationships behind the scenes
of modern medical life are:

### PRIZE OF GOLD
#### *by Hazel Fisher*

It was the eminent surgeon, Sir Carlton Hunter, who
told Sandie that love was the prize of gold — but she
was determined to win the gold medal for the best
student nurse, rather than lose her heart!
Unfortunately, it was also Sir Carlton who was wreck-
ing her chances of winning either prize . . . .

### DOCTOR ON BOARD
### (The Path of the Moonfish)
#### *by Betty Beaty*

To meet Paul Vansini at the very beginning of her first
cruise as a hostess aboard the luxury liner *Pallas Athene*,
should have made Cristie Cummings perfectly happy.
And so it might have done, but for Doctor David
Lindsay's cutting remarks!

# Masquerade
## Historical Romances

*Intrigue excitement romance*

### MEETING AT SCUTARI
#### by Belinda Grey

Even Jessica Linton, bored with the triviality of Victorian society, was not prepared to flout convention by having an affair with a married man. So, to forget her love for Prince Paul Varinsky, she embarked for Scutari in the Crimea, as one of Florence Nightingale's staff, and found herself with the army that was fighting Paul's countrymen . . .

### THE DEVIL'S ANGEL
#### by Ann Edgeworth

Why should Mistress Prue Angel seem so reluctant to encourage the handsome, rakish Duke of Carlington after chance throws them together? The Duke was certainly known throughout Georgian London as the Perfidious Devil, and renowned for his *amours,* but could an unknown like Prue afford to spurn his advances?

Look out for these titles in your local paperback shop from 8th August 1980